The Tidemaster

Linda Mann started writing poetry in the dead hours of the night after her first child was born and progressed to children's plays, scripts for radio and then complete novels. Her first book *Mist* was published in 2001, closely followed by a second in the Tavistock Allan Mystery series.

In 2005 she set up Priory Press Ltd to publish her own books and it has now grown up and become a fully fledged publishing pygmy with nearly twenty writers on its books.

Other books by Linda Mann published by Priory Press:

Mr Boots
The Corsican Trap
The Chronicles of Edwin Snipe

edited by Linda Mann:
A Tail for All Seasons, Volume 1
A Tail for All Seasons, Volume 2

The Tidemaster

Linda Mann

Priory Press

Published by Priory Press Ltd
The Priory, Abbots Way, Abbotswood,
Ballasalla, Isle of Man IM9 3EQ

www.priory-press.co.uk

First published 2003, revised edition 2010

ISBN 978-0-9551510-6-4

Edited and typeset by
Frances Hackeson Freelance Publishing Services,
Brinscall, Lancs
Printed in Great Britain by
Bell and Bain Ltd, Glasgow

Chapter 1

MEMO TO JANICE CORNWALL,
LION PRODUCTIONS

The Glashton

Was a monster from the deep, web-footed and grotesquely featured, who prowled the coastline of the Isle of Man and preyed on young virgins.

He would transform himself with perfumes and rich clothes into a handsome young buck and with promises of jewels, dresses and marriage lure them to the nearest secluded beach. Once there he would overpower his victim and drag her into the sea.

The victim was never seen again and no trace was ever found of either the Glashton or his potential bride.

Quite a good story don't you think? With more than adequate opportunity for major scenes of gratuitous breast-heaving and bodices being ripped! According to my sources he was fairly active for a short while and then all traces of him disappeared. As with most legends there is a lot of material here for your usual taste in stretching the truth. Dare I mention that joy of artistic licence, Nessie and the Wolf boy? Thought you could use the idea in that 'Supernatural Creatures and Legends' series for Channel Four.

Good luck and do let me know if you're interested.

Regards

Sam Lawrence

Chapter 2

453 AD

"NO, oh God no!" A scream of terror, high-pitched and horrified.

He could feel the intense cold and the darkness stretching out and up. He could sense her terror and then he listened, silently hugging himself, as he heard the furtive scrabbling as she tried desperately to find a way out of the nightmare.

There was a stifled sob as she fell and then a scream.

Any moment now and she would begin to realise what the floor of her tomb was made of.

The creature against the wall waited as the sobs changed to a soft keening wail.

'Soon,' he thought, 'the pleading and begging will begin.' For a fleeting moment he wondered whether to let this one go, after all she had been kind to him once. Just once he had received a smile and not a curse, a soft word and not a kick or even worse, stones. He rubbed a patch of scabby skin and scowled. Other memories flooded in and the scowl darkened. She was one of them after all. She was free to walk in the light; free to find love. His had to be snatched. Maybe he would just use her and not eat the remains – but then he would be hungry again and he'd have to catch another. It was taking longer each time to ensnare the unwary. Even now they were beginning to weave stories around him and warning their young to be on their guard. Was this what he had come to? Was he after all really just a monster to frighten children with?

"I could have been great," he half muttered to himself as he remembered the old druid who had promised him so much.

"Who is that?" she whispered, hearing him sigh.

He answered her pleading voice with silence.

"Please, please, I want to go home. Look, I'll help you. Please – it's so cold. You promised me, you promised me ..."

The voice trailed off. Grey silence and the slow drip, drip of cold water from the slate above.

Yes he had promised something, although he couldn't remember what it was. There had been so many promises and the result was always the same: death.

He was tired and the usual shiver of anticipation ending in the stiffening and engorging of his member was slow and sluggish.

Slowly he passed his tongue over his own pale thin lips. He could taste the salt and suddenly felt a need for the warmth of human contact.

All he had ever wanted was to be hugged, to feel the embrace of another.

"It isn't my fault!" he screamed.

The wet walls reverberated with the sound and the girl, knowing now who he was, sank to the floor.

Then the silence settled around them, as dust will in an airless room.

"Oh God help me, Mannanan help me, please help me."

A prayer caught in the back of a throat drying despite the damp.

These Manxies believed in their God, a mythical guardian, but then they believed in fairies and a black dog of death.

She was on her knees now, head bent in an attitude of prayer, damp cloth clinging to the curves he'd coveted for so long. The little shepherdess, auburn hair blowing in the wind, singing to the sheep she protected.

He listened and waited, reluctant to move. Now that she was here, completely unprotected, he found that he didn't want her.

Not like this, not here.

There had been a time, long ago when ...

But he had to have something or he would die; already the sharp pangs of starvation gnawed and nibbled at his stomach reminding him of his own internal needs.

This one he would drown quickly.

As he reached out to take the long tresses of her hair he realised that the air was lightening and that he could dimly see.

Slowly she sat up and looked towards the far wall of rock, her head turned away from him. Startled, he stared as she did at the roughly calloused slab of slate and marbled stone. They watched as a steady stream of vapour crept from the water, black and bottomless, which guarded the cave's mouth. With a mounting sense of unease the crouching predator began to back slowly towards the dark pool, webbed feet splayed against the bone and pebbles. There was the soft sound of liquid rippling and closing over him as he dived down into the cold, dark, salted water, eager to escape the growing light which threatened to blind his weak red eyes.

A figure began to rise from the mist. Cloaked in dark russet, a staff held out in front of him. Dark, almost black eyes burnt in deep-set sockets, merciless, hardened by years of war.

The girl ran to him, clutching at his cloak, crying and laughing and shivering.

He murmured something and held her close.

"Did you think I'd abandon you, my fair one, my sweet Elaine?" he asked.

She shook her head as tears coursed quietly down her face.

Turning from her, the man moved towards the water and waited.

Coughing and spluttering, the creature re-emerged, anger tightened his sinews and made the reed-like voice shrill with indignation.

"What have you done?"

"Sealed your larder, dark one."

"You have no right, no right."

"I have every right to protect my people from your foul feeding. Did you think you could thrive unprotected under my very nose?"

"Who are you, magician or madman?"

"My name is Mannanan Mac Lir and I am your executioner."

"You don't have the power, no one does."

"True, but then I have the Christian God with me."

Mannanan smiled and slowly withdrew a dark wooden cup from the folds of his cloak. It glowed and glinted. Its dark highly polished surface seemed to catch every ray of light. A red aura the colour of newly spilt blood crept along the ground and up the walls, and as it did, the bones beneath their feet shivered and dissolved, slowly merging with black sand and gravel. Mist glimmered and within the silvered folds, figures moved and floated ever upwards.

The creature backed against the wall, fighting the scarlet vapour already seeping slowly into his lungs, chilling his blood and freezing him from within.

"What is that?"

"A cup, a wooden cup. Plain and strong fashioned by a carpenter for a King," Mannanan sighed and placed it reverently on a rocky ledge.

"It will stay here, while up above in the land of light and sunshine, men will die in search of it and you, my foul goblin, will guard it with your dust. I warned you not to bring your vile practices to my land, your death is of your own making, to starve or drown in your own lair."

The creature screamed and flung himself at Mannanan. Disorientated by the light and the mist he reached for the man and the girl, clutching pebbles and dank oily black kelp. With a howl of rage he realised that he was alone. All that remained was the softly glowing cup and the slow, monotone drip, drip of ice-cold water.

* *

Later two men walked along the cliff path. Their bare feet made not a sound on the soft, rabbit mown grass. High above them a solitary black bird fought the winds.

One was a holy man with a shaved, tonsured head and a heavy cross of silver. His face, lined and weathered by the elements, still held that quiet look of patrician authority. He had the look and the olive skin of a Roman. The other, cloaked in velvet the colour of peat, had the tanned leather flesh of a sailor. Sharp brown eyes, the eyes of a hawk, glinted from under bushy grey eyebrows. And hair silvered by the sun and approaching middle age, hung in long wisps against the sharp bones of his face. Both men leant against the wind on strong staffs, one topped with the carved head of some fabulous sea monster, the other embellished with a snake, which looped and arched around the dark, ebony-coloured wood.

"You sealed it well?"

"Yes."

"And the cup?"

"Is now protected by a spirit as cruel as the cup is

good."

"That is as it was ordained. You have done well my friend."

"I could not have succeeded without the woman agreeing to bait the trap."

"And for that I will ensure she has the protection of the men who will come after me."

"She may not agree to follow your new God."

"That is her decision."

They both stopped and looked across the sea towards the Mountains of Mourne.

Turning from his companion, the monk stooped and picked a deep purple-hued wild violet from the ground and after rubbing the petals between his fingers, bent to drink in the perfume he had released.

"I must leave now and travel back before the scribes have missed me and my business with you becomes more than the stuff of legends and fairy tales."

"I will uphold my end of the bargain."

"Then there is little to discuss. Have you told the woman?"

"Not yet."

"You have until the sun sets."

"Thank you."

"It is little enough, for what you have done, and if you should ever need my help ..."

"I will call upon you."

They moved apart then, the monk towards the beach below and the waiting boat, its single sail gently dancing in the freshening wind. His companion watched him go as his long strides took him quickly down to the sheltered inlet of gently swelling waves and moving sand. Mannanan waited until the little craft had turned into the wind ready for its return journey to the northern Irish coast and with a deep sigh, moved towards the golden gorse-strewn hills above. Watching them and seated upon a white marbled rock sat the auburn-haired Elaine, her green eyes shaded by hands still shaking with fear and cold. By her side a shaggy, wolf-like dog panted.

She waited until Mannanan had reached her side and then moved the cloth of her gown to allow him to sit beside her.

"He is leaving then?"

"Aye."

"He is a godly man, for all his piety and soft looks."

"As tough as granite, as are all Romans. Elaine, I must speak with you."

"And here we are, so speak, my own love."

"Did the creature – did it harm you in any way?"

"No, he did no harm that time will not heal."

"Good."

"What was it? I caught a glimpse of white skin and hair, red eyes and webbed feet, unlike any creature I have ever seen."

"He was a boy once but an unwanted one. He was left when but a child to live or die wild amongst the rocks. The monks said he had terrorised the people for many years until they caught him and threw him from their shores. A pity he ended here. Still, he's gone now and will never more roam the cliffs and glens to entice his victims to their dark death."

"Would he have?" She shuddered at the thought of those damp hands upon her. That skin entwined with hers.

"Oh yes, he was like a cat playing with a mouse. First the rape and then the feasting while still warm."

"Feasting?"

"Why do you think he chose the young? He chose as we would choose lamb over mutton, a young plump chicken over a fowl only fit for boiling. The good Patrick said he acquired a taste for human flesh from the cooking pots of

Druids running from the might of Roman wrath."

Elaine sat silently, thoughts of what might have been her fate twisting and writhing in her imagination. Quickly she blinked back the shuddering horror she could feel creeping along the edge of her skin.

"I knew you would come. I prayed you would have the power to find me and to defeat him," she stated, her voice unnaturally bright.

"I had the power to find but the battle was won not by the old laws but by the new. The Roman gave me something to bury with him. That alone has the power to hold his spirit and to eventually redeem his life and death. Without it we would all have perished, trapped within the living rock."

"But you succeeded." She watched his face, her desperate need for reassurance that all was well deepening her voice. He turned from her then, his eyes bright with unshed pain and longing. Now he would have to tell her of the bargain he had had to make, a bargain made to keep her safe.

"At a price."

"A price?"

"I will die, my earthly form will rot but my spirit will be allowed to stay to guard this land from the madness which will devour and divide across the waters. For a thousand years and then another I can stay to roam the hills and glens. I must not intervene if by doing so I counteract this new God. For Him I forfeit all my rights."

He stared out across the warm evening vista of trees, hills and deep purple-blue water. Drinking in the shrill cries of the gulls soaring above him in the gathering dust. He knew why the monk had wanted to hide the cup but now with so little time left he felt the first sharp stabs of regret.

"When will you go?" she asked, watching his face as if intent on memorising every line and curve.

"At sunset."

"Then we still have time," she whispered, and suddenly earnest she turned and taking his strong face between her hands, pressed her lips against his with a passion she had never let him feel before. "I know a space between the rocks, high in the hills, guarded by the hawks and soft with heather and moss. There we can lie together and I will hold your seed within me. Perhaps one day our ancestors will talk with you again and help you in your task."

He held her gaze, knowing better than she of the risk she intended to take.

"Are you sure?" The elders and the priests will call you whore. It is not a good life for you or the child, to be unwed." Still cautious, still prudent but aching to hold her, he pushed her away.

"That will be my decision as it is my body that will hold the child, my pain and my loss. Come, there have been enough words already and my flesh aches and burns for yours."

Her green eyes bore into his with an intensity that startled them both.

He nodded, and catching her small hands in his kissed the knuckles of each hand.

Later as the day darkened, hawks flew and screamed above their bed of leaves. The dog lay stretched across the entrance of their scented bower and watched the sky, oblivious to the soft moans and cries of his mistress.

As the insect-laden dusk began to fall, Mannanan silently wrapped his cloak about him and left the now spent form of the woman he had loved. Above him the sun began to sink, a red ball drowning in a sea of fire. Slowly, drinking in the last sights, sounds and scents of the Island he loved, Mannanan walked, without a single backward glance, down towards the sea. From the deepening shadows of the gorse-rimmed cliffs Elaine watched as he waded slowly through the waves and as the black night crept across the stilled water, cried silent tears as he disappeared beneath the foam.

Chapter 3

Mannanan lifted old eyes towards the dark clouds rushing in from Scotland and turned, as a small child launched himself from the top of a dry stone wall. The previous year he had discovered friends and enemies as he'd protected the Island once more from the old beliefs. Three live souls could see him now, the mother of the child he was with, the child himself and his one direct descendant, Detective Inspector Robert Callow.

He sighed deeply and George turned from the speculative eyeing of a sheep with a concerned frown.

"You all right, Uncle Mac?"

"What? Oh yes George, I'm fine. Just remembering the old days."

"Oh." There was a soft pause as George digested the remark, and deciding that it was irrelevant dismissed it with the comment, "Mum says there was no such thing as the good old days, that it's a myth thought up by people who can't face reality."

"She's probably right," Mannanan mused, still staring upwards.

"Do you think Uncle Bob will ever get his pilot's licence?" George asked, following his gaze.

"What?"

"Uncle Bob. He's up there, trying to fly. I thought that was what you were looking at."

"Oh. How can you tell that it's him?"

"Wing wobble. Look."

Mannanan turned to look to where George was pointing with a short, grime-encrusted index finger. High above the hills and glens a small, white, single-engine plane buzzed and dipped. Mannanan waved to the small metal bird and George shook his head in the superior disbelief of the young faced with the mental aberrations of the elderly.

"He can't see us from up there, you know."

"Ah well, no harm in waving anyway just to be polite."

George frowned, his brows arching. Grown-ups were without exception really weird and he would never understand them, even if he lived to be two hundred years old, or at least well past thirty. Then as sudden inspiration struck, he ran off, hands outstretched.

"George!"

"I'm a plane – Uncle Mac look! I'm a plane."

Mannanan chuckled and followed in George's wake, "Now I know how a sheepdog feels. From deity to babysitter," he thought.

"How the mighty have fallen." A faceless voice, now long dead and almost forgotten hissed. Mannanan spun towards the sound. His mind reached outwards and searched the surrounding air without success, but all he felt was a finger of dread tracing the bony curve of his spine.

***

Detective Inspector Bob Callow chuckled inwardly like the ten-year-old boy he felt himself to be, not the middle-aged policeman he outwardly was and flew straight through the hole in the centre of a white fluffy cloud in front of the perspex screen. Coming out the other side, Bob viewed the patchwork pattern of fields holding together the northern plain and banked sharply to the right. Tim, his instructor, inhaled nosily and shook his head in mock despair.

"Bob, you couldn't just keep to our original heading could you? Only it's easier to teach if I don't feel that what you really want to do is buzz sheep on the slopes of Snaefell, and terrorise the local rabbit population, not learn how to fly."

"Sorry Tim, I just had this uncontrollable urge."

"Yeah, right, well I've heard about them but I'd rather discuss it later when we're both on good old terra firma. Anyway now that you've got that out of your system and every farmer for miles has rung in and complained, I'll show you what the rudder is supposed to do …"

As Tim patiently explained, pointing out the necessary instruments, Bob endeavoured to listen, his brain struggling to keep up with the growing plethora of data whilst avoiding overload. Twenty minutes later as they turned to head back towards the Island's airport, Bob thought he caught a glimpse of someone brown-cloaked and familiar striding across the high hills.

"So to go down you do this, eh?" Bob asked, pushing down with the stick whilst keeping one eye on the rapidly descending altimeter, its small hand moving quickly anti-clockwise. The plane juddered.

"What?" Tim shouted. "No! Do it gently, we don't want to stall."

"What's that then?" Bob grinned.

"The engine cuts out, not good when you only have one of them to start with."

"See Tim, one lesson with me and your sense of humour is coming back."

"And my breakfast! Bob, steady on – do you have any

idea what it would cost to replace this?"

Bob began to descend at a gentler rate as he banked and circled towards the ground. Thermals caught at the wings and the plane bucked in the air like a live thing. Below Bob could clearly see the brown-robed figure and waved. The figure waved back and the child standing behind him shaded his eyes with his hands against the glowing sun and the bright, silver-rimmed clouds.

Tim, looking down, muttered. "If that woman doesn't hurry up, her kid will be away over the hills before she can catch up."

Bob looked over to where Tim was pointing to the rounded figure of a green-jacketed, tartan-skirted female who appeared to be vainly pulling on the lead of a large black dog. The woman also looked up and the dog sat. Bob realised belatedly that Tim could very obviously not see the rather elderly gentleman beside the boy and as they began to climb up towards a safer altitude he listened with only half an ear, as Tim waxed lyrical on parental lack of control and juvenile delinquency.

As they raced across the sky Bob took one last look at the brown stick-like figure of Mannanan Mac Lir and exhaled noisily.

"What's up?" Tim asked noting, both the sound and the whitening of knuckles around the Joystick.

"Nothing, just someone walking over my grave."

"Oh." There was a thoughtful pause. "Right, well in that case we'd better find you something to take your mind off it. I think it's high time we pottered back to Ronaldsway and I can explain with the aid of a few very large charts and some really thick textbooks just exactly what sort of things you'll have to learn before being able to obtain your basic pilot's licence."

"Textbooks?"

"What did you think you had to do? Buzz a few sheep,

frighten the life out of me and learn to be rude to air traffic? No, if you really want your licence you're going to have to work at it and that includes written examinations." Tim smiled, the sadist in him enjoying Bob's obvious lack of enthusiasm towards the very thought of anything involving voluntary paperwork.

"And then when we get back we'll go through your pre-flight checks, add a bit of air law, some meteorology and sort out your obvious problems with vectors," he added maliciously.

"Oh," Bob mumbled in reply, his joy in the day diminishing fast.

***

The woman in the green jacket continued to march across the rich flower-strewn hillside as the circling plane disappeared from view, the noise remaining for some time afterwards.

"We just don't have that kind of money."

The words rolled around her head, again and again. Stopping suddenly, she searched in her pockets for a cigarette. Turning her body against the wind, she lit it with a gold Cartier lighter and drew the hot, bitter smoke deep down into her lungs. Again she dug into her pocket and this time extracted a thin blue page of closely typed print.

> Please find enclosed newspaper cuttings concerning the death of an internee during the time of your father's secondment to the island. Nothing in it you think? Then take a long look at the copied sheets of a notebook found amongst a relative's effects. It might be interesting to hear what the press would say, especially if you take into account the political climate in Europe at this time. Scapegoats are such unhappy people. A rumour here, a well placed e-mail there.

I do have more evidence and a wish, not unnatural, for the finer things in life. Why don't we meet and discuss a one-off payment of say ... one hundred thousand pounds? Think of it as an insurance policy and a small price to pay for silence and the continuance of a glittering career.

After all they do say 'like father, like son!'

I will let you know when and where.

It was all there, treason, theft and murder. If the copied sheets she held in her hand were only half true. She bit down on her lip, hard enough to break the skin and in so doing, released a single drop of blood.

It was all so long ago and so many of those involved were now dead. Surely no one cared?

"Except the relatives of the deceased," prompted the dark voice of her inner self.

She could at a pinch raise the money but it would take time; time and a lot of lying. Or she could lay the whole thing in front of the one man who would know the truth.

She ground her teeth in frustration and stared balefully at the ground.

There was another choice and that was to meet the blackmailer and persuade him or her to let it go.

A child screamed joyously into the wind, arms outstretched, coat billowing behind him.

She closed her eyes briefly as if in pain and then, her final decision made, turned on her heel and headed back towards the wooded glen shading the road below.

Above her a woman's voice called to the boy, now out of sight, amongst the grey stone walls and banks of yellow gorse and purple heather. The dog wheezed at her side, struggling for breath against the too tight collar, as she half pulled, half dragged the elderly beast back to her waiting car.

Mannanan watched her stride back towards her vehicle, his concern for her an uneasy feeling of damp hitting arthritic joint. For some reason she had the air of one either damned or doomed.

As if sensing his temporary self-absorption, George suddenly jumped out at him from the precarious lip of a dry stone wall and landed catlike at his feet.

"George," Mannanan moaned, picking the small child up and brushing the worst of the grey dust from his clothes. "I do wish you'd at least try to look where you leap."

"I'm a plane," George replied. "It was a crash landing. You expect bits to fall off when you crash. Besides, you should have caught me!"

Mannanan glared at him, his emotions caught between laughter and the strong desire to pick him up and deposit him off the end of a small cliff.

It was at that point that Tavistock Allan arrived to reclaim her son, with the soothing words, "George, how on earth did you get another hole in those new trousers, I only bought them a week ago?" George, suddenly stricken, looked down at the offending garment and sighed.

"It wasn't me," he muttered.

"Who was it then, the invisible man and a pair of scissors?" Clearly exasperated, Tavistock moved towards him, hands held in front of her as if she were ready to throttle him. Then before he could retaliate she grabbed him and planted a bright pink lipstick kiss on his cheek and ruffled his hair with the palm of her hand. George grimaced and moving quickly away, began to plaster the strands of hair back down with his own spit after carefully wiping all signs of her affection from his face.

"Oh my poor baby, don't you want to give your mummy a big kiss back then? How about a lovely hug, for your tired mumsie? Just a little one?" Tavistock grinned.

"Oh Yuk! Gross. You know I hate it when you go all sloppy. What if anyone had seen! It's so embarrassing." George moved quickly to the side of the path and scowled ferociously.

"If the wind changes, you'll stay like that," Mannanan told him.

"Really? Cool!" George turned into the wind and screwed his features into something closely resembling a cathedral gargoyle.

Mannanan laughed and turned towards Tavistock who was now studiously ignoring her small son. "So how did your day in the heady world of cinematography go?"

"Cine what?" George asked, moving closer, as he was now being totally ignored by both adults.

Tavistock emitted a deep huffing sound between her teeth and Mannanan patted her gently on the shoulder.

"I gather the day was not a success," he stated, observing the sudden mulish look in her eyes.

"You could say that," Tavistock replied, staring intently down at a black glossy beetle, which had just skittered over her left shoe before diving into the grass. "To be perfectly honest, I have no idea why they want a writer present. The idiot who calls himself a director changes everything at least twice before the actors see the final draft but only if the poor things have actually learnt the lines in the first place. Then they hang around drinking tea while the light changes from terrible to appalling and then five minutes into the thirty-fourth take 'Brain of Britain' decides he doesn't like the ending and you have to sit down and start all over again. A scriptwriter for the 'Teletubbies' or 'Bob the Builder' would have a better chance of lucidity. I mean, it's a film about local legends, not a remake of 'Gone with the Wind'."

Mannanan and George looked at each other, their faces registering the same blank expression.

"Gone with the ... what?" George asked. Mannanan shook his head and gave George's hand a warning squeeze.

Irritated, Tavistock glared at them both before turning and heading back down towards her car, which was basking gently in the warm afternoon sunshine like a large olive-green seal.

"Anyway, I quit!" She shouted back at them without breaking her stride.

"Oh!" Mannanan and George uttered in unison. Mannanan moved quickly to her side and after checking her face to see if she really minded, was reassured by the malicious grin spreading across her features.

"And now they'll have to bring someone over from the mainland and that will really please the accountants!" Tavistock gleefully declared, rubbing her hands together in a satisfied fashion. "Right then, who wants to go to The Paparazzi for tea, as I don't have to pick the girls up until later?" Tavistock asked.

"Me, Me, Me!" shrieked George happily.

Tavistock and Mannanan walked sedately back towards the car, George following in their wake, hands held stiffly at his sides, his gait that of a strange sideways waddle.

"Does he need to, er, go somewhere?" Mannanan enquired.

"Nope, he's being a penguin. They've got some new ones down at the Wildlife Park."

"Ah," Mannanan said. "He was a plane earlier on."

"Last week he wanted to be a Viking and the week before that a South American hissing cockroach."

"Well at least he's consistent," Mannanan laughed, suddenly remembering long-dead adversaries. "So, which legends are they digging up this year? There are a few skeletons it would be as well not to disturb. Perhaps I am one of them?"

They both laughed, and the small boy looked up and frowned. Grown-ups, especially old ones, were still a big mystery and almost certainly mad.

"The Glashton," she replied, carefully avoiding a small clutch of ink-black rabbits' droppings.

Mannanan stopped, stunned. Thoughts and memories whirling, old wounds reopening, long- forgotten sorrows reawakened.

"Why that tale?" Mannanan muttered, his throat suddenly dry and constricted.

"Don't know. The powers that be preferred it to the Black Dog of Peel and the Buggane I suppose. Does it matter?"

"No, I don't suppose it does, not now."

The full truth no one would ever know. He'd made sure of that, when he'd buried it alive, within the walls of the Chasms.

And if ...

No, it was impossible that it should ever escape, impossible and unthinkable.

Chapter 4

The L'Experience restaurant was nearly full. A babble of voices filled the room, growing in direct correlation to the amount of alcohol being consumed. Wafts of garlic and herbs steamed from plates held aloft by scurrying waitresses. Above the gently glowing candles, small white bulbs glinted from a suspended ceiling of thin wooden laths and dark green foliage.

Harold Erskine ate, silently chewing each mouthful and swallowing as quietly as he could, his eyes riveted to the plate in front of him. His companion sat, arms folded, a scowl fixed rigidly to a fat, unhandsome face, food untouched upon the plate before her. She nodded once, as the plate was removed and a fresh one placed upon the red and white tablecloth in front of her. Harold raised his eyes furtively as she took a careful sip of wine. The scowl darkened and her fingers drummed a dirge of displeasure, the heavy ornate rings on her fingers sparkling and glistening as multi-faceted gems caught and held the light.

Harold, who had already consumed his glass of Fleurie, quaked inwardly. It was always the same when they ate out. The starter was never quite right. This time it was the allegedly 'undercooked aubergine', last time it had been the smell of fish and the time before that the chef had used too much pepper. Harold sighed. 'She would,' he thought, 'send back a dish prepared by Anton Mossiman himself.' The wine would be corked. It always was. Or it would be too warm or too cold. There would, undoubtedly, be something wrong with either or both of the next two courses and she would then grumble incessantly about the bill. He quickly poured himself another glass of wine and drank it hurriedly. The way he coped was to drink. Drink and eat in quiet abject misery. Alone inside his head he dreamed of freedom. Secretly he plotted to become a real life Reggie Perrin. He would leave his old self on a lonely stretch of beach and escape to Scotland and become a gentleman of the road or maybe he'd strike lucky become a Mr Polly. Harold scowled at his plate, scooping up the remains of the lamb's lettuce. Other people managed it, other men of his own age who left without trace and were swallowed up by the world. He'd seen it on the news and secretly rejoiced, as he had as a young man when he watched Steve McQueen throwing a baseball in the cooler and knew that next time he'd really do it – escape!

There was a snort of almost bovine proportions from his companion. Studiously he avoided the openly sympathetic looks he was beginning to receive from the other patrons. 'They ought to just ask us to leave,' he thought bitterly. 'It would save everyone the hell of the inevitable final showdown, the settling of the bill.'

"Mona," he hissed despairingly. "I'm sure the wine is fine, look – I'm drinking it."

His wife glared at him from cold, malevolent, grey eyes.

"You would drink vinegar if it contained alcohol!" she snorted, openly derisive, her words coated in vitriol.

Harold gave up and stuffed the last succulent Queenie into his mouth. A globule of garlic butter ran down his chin.

"You are such a disgusting little man," stated his wife as she began to dissect the substitute starter, the aubergine slice which sat smoking gently on the carefully dressed plate in front of her now chargrilled to the point of inedibility.

Harold sighed heavily and sank further into his chair, his neck almost disappearing into the freshly laundered collar of his immaculate bespoke shirt.

Without warning, he remembered a time when he used to read to his youngest daughter. One of her favourite books, was Roald Dahl's Charlie and the Great Glass Elevator. Glancing surreptitiously at Mona he began to see a more than striking resemblance between his wife and a large Vermicious Knid. This resemblance became overwhelming as Mona glared malignantly at her plate. A chuckle began to well up within Harold's slight frame. Without realising he grinned broadly. A man sitting opposite caught his eye and smiled back, the simple understanding look of male comradeship. Harold felt himself blushing and a sudden mad desire to tip the plate of food over his wife and walk out, thundered in his head. Thirty years ago he might have done it, when he still had a job, when he was still financially independent, before she had inherited the money. Maybe if he had walked out earlier he'd still have children that talked to him and grandchildren he was allowed to see. Tears of self-pity welled and rapidly he blinked them away. He drank the remaining ruby-red liquid and poured the last of the bottle into his glass.

***

Bob Callow continued watching the middle-aged couple for a moment more and then turned back to Moira.

"When was the last time I told you that I loved you?" he asked, picking up a large serving spoon before helping himself to the creamed spinach, heavily garlic-laden and delicious.

"This morning," Moira replied, eyes twinkling. Bob grinned at her, remembering. He had finally taken a morning off from work, which had meant there had been no need to answer the telephone, no need to hide from the children both now safely at university and no need to put any clothes on.

"And yes dear," Moira continued, "if I ever treat you like that, you can take me outside and shoot me." Moira glared at the woman opposite, raising her voice just enough to be heard by those concerned and at least half the surrounding restaurant.

"No, my love I don't think I'd shoot you, I'd just leave and take the cat with me," Bob declared, taking a sip of perfectly chilled sparkling wine.

There was a general wave of tittering and a few veiled smiles as the other diners tried not to look at the middle-aged couple. The woman, enraged, glared at Moira who stared haughtily back. Losing the battle of wills, Mona turned to her companion and informed him that they were leaving. Harold sighed. He'd been really looking forward to his fillet steak with the special lady-killer sauce and as for having to leave the little pot of chocolate mousse again … well it just wasn't fair. A tiny spark of rebellion flared briefly.

Moira winked at Harold. A man sitting in the corner coughed into his handkerchief and began an earnest discussion with his scantily clad companion. Harold wondered if they were married. "Of course they aren't," said that small sly voice in his head. "They're still talking to each other." The voice sniggered, a bitter reminder of a Harold long gone.

Harold shrugged himself into his expensive Austin Reed jacket. As he did he caught sight of Bob touching Moira's cheek with the tip of his finger, an unhurried intimate gesture. Harold felt a barb of envy, small but steel-tipped. His wife wrapped her long fur coat around her and walked out, head held high, lips thinly pursed, only two red spots on her sallow cheeks giving the lie to the fact that Moira's well-aimed comments had struck home.

Mona drove their recently acquired large, white Mercedes home in frigid upright silence. Harold sat in the passenger seat and concentrated on keeping relatively upright.

Trees and walls blurred as the car picked up speed along the winding country roads. Cottages and farmhouses squatted damply amid the hills and glens, their welcoming squares of yellow light beacons to other luckier homecomers. Home – how warm a single word could sound. His home, he mused bitterly, was just somewhere he slept and ate in, no more and no less. At last the walls and gates loomed ahead out of the enveloping darkness. Mona accelerated towards the shadowed house, tyres biting into the drive, scattering small rounds of gravel like shrapnel onto the surrounding lawn.

Harold's hands trembled slightly as he aimed the remote at the garage. Double aluminium doors moved smoothly upwards to reveal a large dark cavern. Harold was reminded of the entrance to a dragon's mouth in one of his ancient schoolbooks and barely repressed a shudder. Blue light flickered as the overhead striplights came on and the cavern was revealed to be just an ordinary empty space of grey concrete and white, newly painted shelves.

"I don't see why you want to set up a workshop in here," Mona complained, cutting the engine.

"I thought it would give me something to do, dear."

"Do? You never do anything, you never did!" Mona spluttered, her dark eyes sparkling with barely concealed hatred.

"I thought I could have a lathe in here and make things." Harold's eyes lit up at the prospect, the small flame of independence quenched almost at birth by a single look from his wife.

"Do what you want," Mona shrugged and began to move to the inside door which separated the garage from the rest of the house.

"I think I'll take the dog out for a walk along the beach. If that's all right, dear?" Harold asked. "It's a nice evening," he added. Nervously he adjusted his tie, a small movement, which never failed to do anything but irritate his wife.

"Do what you like, I'm going to bed."

"Do you want me to join you?" Harold asked tentatively.

"Don't be disgusting, you can sleep in the spare room. You stink of garlic and you've been drinking, which means you will snore. You always do. Besides I have a charity lunch tomorrow and I need to look my best." Dismissing her husband with the same clipped tone of voice she would have used with the daily or the gardener, she opened the connecting door and stomped loudly away out of sight, her expensive leather shoes clicking angrily across the polished stone floor of the adjoining kitchen.

Harold remained standing by the car until the overhead noises of footsteps and the sound of running water stopped. Surreptitiously he removed a lid from an empty can of white gloss paint, secreted in a corner by the garage doors and checking once more that all was clear, removed a packet of cigarettes and a lighter. Carefully he replaced the lid and whistled for his dog.

"Sally, Sally, here girl." The dog, which had raced from the interior of the garage as soon as it had opened and was now busily digging up one of the front rosebushes, launched herself back into the garage, tail wagging and jaws drooling. Harold dropped to his knees and rubbed her soft shaggy ears and tummy as the small brown and white animal rolled ecstatically at his feet. Sally was his dog, a gift from his daughter before her move to Canada. He could still remember the way she had pushed the warm bundle of fur into his arms before he'd waved his last farewell at the airport.

Sadly he hugged Sally to him. He didn't care that she had parentage that even the vet had hesitated to even guess at, or that she dropped hairs everywhere and terrorised the aged gardener. Sally loved him.

"Harold!" shouted a voice from above.

Harold quickly gathered up a lead from a selection hanging from a nail stuck into the new shelves and slithered out, Sally now quiet, hugging his heels.

At the bottom of the drive they stopped and looked back at the house. Harold pressed the remote and slipped it back in his pocket. The garage doors slunk back into place and the darkened house glared balefully down at them.

Finally on reaching the main road, Harold felt like cheering. He was free and if he hurried he could get a quick half in at the Bee's Knees before closing. Harold smiled, suddenly happy. He had escaped with his trusty hound and a whole packet of Bensons.

Later he would take a walk to the quiet secluded bay he called his own and dream of faking his own death.

***

Barney Goldsmith huddled into the folds of his anorak and stared out at the blank expanse of water. A polystyrene cup cartwheeled across the beach and banked against his foot before hurling itself back into the wind and disappearing into the night. He could hear footsteps from the road above and looked up. A dog barked and was quickly silenced by a distant whispered admonishment. The voice lurched between registers, the consonants blurred. 'Someone's had a good evening,' Barney thought, a trifle enviously.

He stamped his feet on the uneven stones. It was cold and he was hungry. Concentration slipped as he focused on the night out that he'd missed. Overloaded plates of pasta, litres of Peroni and the chance, if he'd played his cards right, of a bit of horizontal dancing. His stomach rumbled in protest and he raised his wrist to try and see the time. The luminous hands of his watch glowed weakly in the harsh light of a nearly full moon. 'Why couldn't people keep to appointments?' he wondered bitterly. Suddenly inspiration hit. Somewhere in the folds of the anorak he'd borrowed, there was a bar of chocolate. He remembered now grabbing a bar from the pretty blonde on reception.

The dog suddenly began to bark. Pebbles rolled down the slipway towards him, minor avalanches of sound and someone was shouting. Barney froze, unsure, and as he made to move something cold and clammy brushed his cheek. The stench of seaweed and salt made him gag. A strong hand fastened around his neck and he felt himself being pulled towards the sea. Cold water foamed at his feet as the tide washed over his new shoes, darkening the pale cream leather. Stones and sand moved beneath him and he felt the hot tang of bile rise in his throat as the stench of rotting fish reached him. Desperately struggling, he tried to twist away but he overbalanced and fell into ice cold, bone-numbing water. Something was pulling him down as the salt stung his eyes and invaded his nose and mouth. He coughed and choked, inviting yet more seawater into struggling lungs. Above him the dog continued to bark ferociously whilst its companion searched feverishly for the man, who up to that moment had stood on the beach.

Down below the black bubbling waves, Barney gave one last small shudder of flesh and was finally stilled as the spirit fled. The figure clutching him began to swim out towards the headland, dragging its dead cargo of cloth and flaccid skin with it.

Harold, tears streaming down his face, continued to search the shoreline. Panic tore at his body. Nerves battered by years of marriage began to send frantic contradictory messages. Eventually the dog and its master began the steep climb back towards the village and the nearest phone.

Below him two sets of footprints rapidly filled with blotched, white water and softly merged, their individuality disappearing back into the flattening wave-drenched sandy beach.

It was almost as if the Island itself had decided to deny the existence of either man or killer.

Chapter 5

July 8th a.m.

Brian Clague groaned inwardly and sincerely wished that the small, incoherent little man in front of him would sober up enough to make even partial sense. The constable standing beside the door wished it too, but was smart enough not to let it show. They had picked Harold Erskine up from the old harbour master's house. He had rung them from there, babbling about murder and water. The dog, caught in its master's hands, was eventually released from Harold's terrified grip and at the moment was tucking into a jam doughnut and a saucer of sweet milky tea. Brian looked down at his cup with something akin to longing and patiently started his questions again.

"So you left the Bee's Knees public house at about eleven?"

"Yes."

"And then?"

"I thought I'd take Sally ..."

"That's the dog?"

"Yes, down the beach for a run. Only when I got there I could see someone standing down near the water's edge."

"Do you remember anything about this person?"

"Well, I thought it was a man."

"Oh?"

"Well he – it – coughed like one. He had what sounded like a sort of smoker's cough, and I think he looked thin, well his legs did. The moon was out and I could see quite clearly to begin with."

"And did you say anything to him?"

"Not then. To be honest I was a bit put out, I mean it's the best time of day down there, at night. No people and Sally can do what she likes without some nosy cow whinging on about dog mess and stuff."

"Right."

"Anyway I was going to go because he looked like he was waiting for someone."

"Oh, and how did you make that out?"

"Dunno, it's just that he just stood there ... oh and he made a movement with his hands, looked like he was trying to look at his watch or something on his wrist. So I turned back and then the moon went behind a cloud and the dog suddenly went mad."

"Mad?"

"Barking and whining, she even gave this weird growl, never heard her like it before. Well, I tried to calm her down but she wouldn't have it. I must have looked back towards the beach over her head and I saw this thing standing behind the man on the beach."

"You mean some person surely?"

"No, I mean thing. It was covered in what looked like some sort of weed and there was this smell, I think that's what Sally smelt. Anyway I started shouting and waving my hands about to warn him – the guy – that it ... and then, and then ..." Harold stopped, the horror in his face still fresh from the memory.

"I saw this thing drag that poor man towards the water and I think he must have tripped. They both fell because I heard a splash and the moon went in behind a cloud. I tried to help. I shouted and called out. Sally and I raced towards him and when the moon came back out – it must have only been a few moments – there was nothing there. Just black water and weed, bits of old rope and things ..."

"Things?"

"Oh I don't know, plastic cups, old net, a child's shoe. Oh, and this." Almost furtively Harold rummaged around in his pockets, finally producing a silver coloured wristwatch. Weed still clung to the metallic strap.

"Looks expensive," Brian observed, carefully dropping it into a plastic evidence bag with the end of his pen.

"It must have been knocked off in the struggle." Harold leant towards Brian, his face eager with the almost desperate desire to be believed.

"It could have been dropped by anyone," Brian replied. "But we'll check anyway. Anything else?"

"No, I ran back towards the first house I could see. Well, you know the rest."

"Yes. Yes I do." Brian paused carefully before continuing. "Look, the thing is, we do know you'd had a few, no one else heard or saw anything. We searched that beach with the proverbial toothcomb. We even had a boat out with flashlights and we found absolutely nothing. And your description of the attacker, it's, well, it's ..." Brian stopped, lost for words.

It was at that moment that the duty sergeant entered with a tray of tea and a clutch of messages. He was also carrying a copy of the local newspaper The Examiner under one arm and as he put the tray down it slipped from his grasp and fell to the floor with a rustle of pages. Harold bent to pick it up and as he did, his faced suddenly blanched. With trembling hands he thrust the page he'd picked up at Brian.

"Look!" he shouted. "That's him. That's what I saw down on the beach – it's him!"

Brian and the sergeant both stared at the page. The

looks they exchanged spoke volumes.

"Why don't you have a nice cup of tea and go home, have a bit of a rest like?" the sergeant said, placing a steaming mug of tea in front of Harold.

"Things always look better in the morning," he added with a conspiratorial wink at Brian.

"But that's him, I tell you that's him!"

"Drink your tea and then we'll give you a lift home," Brian muttered, still staring at the photograph in front of him.

"I don't want to go home! I want you to find that poor man!"

"Right, well as soon as it's light, we'll sort something out. The coastguards have been alerted. We've frankly done all we can for now. You just drink your tea."

Brian sat glaring down at the macabre face, which almost seemed to mock him from the pages of the paper. Harold sat and quietly drank the strong, dark fluid, tears of tiredness and frustration welling in eyes already red from previous weeping.

The young constable at the door moved towards the paper and read the caption to himself.

> The Glashton returns to the Isle of Man in Carlton Television's new thriller series. Look out for his horrifying face on your screens next spring.

There was more about the new series including a few salacious details about the young and well-upholstered female co-star, but the young man remained at Harold's side as he took in the twisted, weed-hung features of the Glashton.

"You saw this grab a strange man and drag him down into the water?" Brian asked.

"Yes, I keep telling you that! Why won't you believe me?"

Sally had finished her milky snack and was now panting quietly at Harold's feet, her saliva dribbling quietly over his salt-encrusted shoes.

"They weren't doing any filming were they? Only they do, you know, because I got an extra part in that 'Frightmare' series. I mean you might not even see the cameras in the dark. They could easily have cleared off before we got there," the young policeman observed.

"It was real, it was." Harold looked around the silent room at his companions. He knew they thought he'd been drinking and with almost sober clarity he could now see why.

There was a brief silence.

"I think I'd like to go home, if you don't mind," Harold muttered, setting his half drunk mug of tea carefully back down onto the table.

"Right," said the sergeant. "I'll give you a lift. I'm off duty in a minute and I go past your place, save you the expense of a taxi, eh?"

"That's very kind of you officer, very kind," Harold replied, rising and at the same time trying desperately to avoid any form of eye contact with anyone.

Brian remained seated long after they'd gone and re-read the accompanying news story. Logic dictated that there was a perfectly simple explanation for what Harold had or hadn't seen but his guts told him something else. Tomorrow he would just pop around to have a quiet confidential word with his immediate superior. After all, Bob Callow may have been on a fortnight's leave but he was always available during daylight hours for a calming cup of tea and the opportunity to down tools. Possibly 'Uncle Bob' would have a few ideas.

***

As Brian sat musing, Cora Cringle the duty coastguard was trying not to throttle Bert Faragher the younger. Bert Faragher the elder sat on a large, lichen-topped rock and drank tea as nosily as he could through ill-fitting dentures. The tea he'd brought himself in an old, tartan-patterned plastic flask. Cora and Juan Qualtrough, the young police constable from Ramsey, had both declined the offer of the restorative beverage on the grounds that the liquid bore more of a resemblance to creosote than to tea. No one was quite sure why Bert the elder had insisted on accompanying his son down to the beach at Garwick, as his son was well into his forties and Bert the elder was on the shady side of sixty. Father and son shared the same weather-hardened features and belligerent attitude to any form of authority but there the similarity ended. Bert the elder was small, slight and bony with angular features and sunken, ferret-like eyes. Bert the younger was tall, balding and had already acquired the rotund beer belly of the single, middle-aged male. Both were toilers of the fields – one from choice, the other because he'd never had any option.

Some fifty feet or so below them, figures in yellow fluorescent waterproofs scoured the beach and the surrounding cliffs with hand-held, heavy-duty torches, their beams giving out a million watts each. Juan had remarked upon the strength of the light being forced into every nook and cranny and Cora, glad of something else to talk about, had described the strength, weight and wattage of the specialised torches. Even Faragher the elder had been impressed, despite his caustic comments and barbed remarks about the taxpayer's money currently being wasted on what was in all likelihood nothing more than a nocturnal seal.

Cora rubbed the tips of her gloved fingers together, a small movement born from a combination of cold and frustration. She looked at her watch and the luminous waterproof dial blinked back at her; it was two thirty in the morning. The policeman standing beside her blew into his hands and stamped his feet in a bid to circulate a little warm blood to the toes that thought his legs had been cut off.

"So, Mr Faragher," Cora said, glaring at Bert the younger. "This body on the beach, you sure it was a body?"

"Yes," Bert the younger snapped. He was tired and a little the worse for drink, and having been up at five the previous morning was in desperate need of more than a few hours' sleep.

"You sure it wasn't a seal?" Faragher senior grinned and his son glared at him.

"No!"

"They do look the same as a body, especially at night."

"Since when did seals wear jeans?" Bert the younger asked, scowling into the freshening wind.

Bert the elder chortled into his plastic cup, spraying warm brown fluid from the corners of his mouth. His son cast him a look that would have soured milk, and Juan, wiping a globule of tarry fluid from his cheek, moved hastily upwind of the now gently cackling old man.

"So, if you were so convinced," Juan asked, pausing to check the contents of his notepad with a small pencil torch. "Why did you drive all the way home, which, by my reckoning must be at least a good ten miles from here, have your dinner and then call us?"

"Dunno, just did," Bert mumbled.

"Bin drinking with that bint of his," Bert the elder hissed, enjoying himself.

"She ain't a bint!" Bert the younger turned and shouted at his father.

"Is!"

"Gentlemen, please." Both men stopped and stared at Cora. Juan muttered "gentlemen" in a questioning tone and was given 'the look'. There was an uneasy silence, into which the sounds of searchers and the sea dropped like pebbles into a pool.

"The point is," Cora continued, daring anyone to interrupt, which nobody had any intention of doing, "we've searched the bay, the surrounding rocks and – nothing. The tide's been in and out since you made up your mind to call us."

"Wouldn't have bothered if I thought it 'ud cause all this," Bert the younger muttered mutinously, whilst not meeting her gaze.

"Well you did," Bert the elder snapped.

There was a burst of static followed by a string of words and sounds from the VHF radio. Cora listened in the gathering silence and then told her men to stand down.

"Nothing – you'd better get off home both of you, and thanks for your help."

The Faraghers took one last look at the beach and walked back up towards the road and their parked Land Rover.

Juan sighed. "Sorry I had you lot out for nothing," he said, trying to keep the tiredness out of his voice.

Cora, who had been staring at the clouds scudding across the moon balanced like a large silver umbrella above their heads, smiled at him. He was young, only a few years older than her eldest boy. To him a body was an excitement. To her, it was the worst part of her job, an unpleasantness to be handled with care and circumspection.

"Don't be, there probably was a body. The wind was fairly light earlier on this evening, probably no more than force two or three. If the body was only a short distance from the beach when it went in, it could easily have been blown onto the shore and then taken out when the tide turned. I'll ask our lads at Ramsey if they can send a patrol out and have a look round Maughold Head and Port Moar.

If there is anything and the wind doesn't change, it might end up there."

"And if the wind changes?" Juan asked, aware that the light breeze was growing in strength as they watched the searchers packing up.

"It's about a four at the moment. If it goes above force five and changes direction from south to south-west, our decomposing cadaver could end up in Scotland. We could get lucky and have a fishing boat pick it up but then we might not get all of it."

"Sorry?"

Cora paused for a brief moment before continuing; he was after all, she thought, very young. "Bodies don't keep and there are an awful lot of carnivores out there. Besides, when you think about it, it seems fair really. We eat them and they eat us – they like the soft bits first. The eyes are the best bits apparently or at least that's what one of my marine biologist friends told me. You ever want to get rid of a body, chop it up, stick it in a lobster pot and hurl it out to sea. Crabs, lobsters, prawns – they love anything soft and meaty."

"Please tell me you're kidding?"

"Nope. You ask Mike there, he had one in England like that. Forensic only managed to identify it because of an old metal hip replacement."

"Hip?"

"Yeah, not the sort of thing you want to find in your crab pots, after a week risking life and limb to reach them." Mike, who had joined them, stated.

"Crustacea don't like metal additives and the joint had a serial number," Cora added helpfully, as they all made their weary way back to their waiting vehicles.

Juan stopped and turned back for one last look at the waves pounding the beach: white curls of light and the sharp shadows of rock receding into salty darkness.

"Will we find it?" he asked.

"Oh yes, eventually," Cora replied. She and Mike exchanged identical looks and then left him, a solitary dark Lowry matchstick shape staring out to sea.

***

The battered old suitcase began another journey along the conveyor belt at Ronaldsway airport. A hunched figure sweeping the marble-patterned floor with a balding broom stopped to watch its now solitary progress. It was a single melancholy item of uncollected plastic.

The throng of businessmen, tourists and locals had gone a few minutes before and the next batch was already on its way, moving towards the baggage reclaim point, in a disorderly mêlée. Old people clutching plastic carriers and wooden sticks, men in charcoal-grey suits, ties loud with individuality, families with children and squawking babies, damp-bottomed and overtired.

The sweeper stopped and moved his back against a wall. Hands deep in pockets, he watched the stampede for trolleys and the thrust of elbows as each traveller tried to pick the best spot beside the black rubber belt, its surface a chain of interlocked flat scales, now silent. The suitcase sat poised halfway round but no one approached it.

A thump sounded as the first of the baggage carts arrived, machinery whirled and the alarm shrilled, assaulting the eardrums as the belt again began to move. Slowly more cases, canvas holdalls, golf bags and children's buggies arrived and were eagerly removed. Hands grabbed and tempers frayed as children squirmed and asked the same tired questions.

With the last traveller gone, the man resumed his sweeping and out of curiosity, if nothing else, moved towards the unclaimed suitcase. As he neared the object of interest, he thought he could smell something, something unpleasantly sweet, the stale stench of a butcher's shop in the heat of summer. A small pool of rust-brown liquid had begun to ooze from the seams and joints of the case.

The man dropped his brush and ran towards the exit, barging into a portly member of security.

"Hold on there, Geoff, where's the fire then?"

"In there. Blood. Gotta have a bit of air, need a fag."

Bemused, the security officer shook his head. Old Geoff had been cleaning floors since the days of the biplane, or at least as long as anyone else had worked there. He turned his ample frame towards the baggage section and spotted the lonely case and then on moving closer, the fluid oozing from its plastic pores.

"Bloody hell!" he exclaimed, rapidly contacting his superior on his mobile and everyone else he could raise.

Minutes later the case was surrounded and alternative arrangements made for the collection of property for the next in-bound flight.

Excitement and an almost ghoulish dread had gripped the bystanders as they waited for a senior member of security to arrive. Finally, convinced that it wasn't going to explode and could be moved, they gingerly transferred the case to a waiting trolley and hastily removed it to a place of safety and better air conditioning.

Bob Callow found his old colleague Dave Shipley in sole charge of the interesting item twenty minutes later. It was now leaking copious quantities of brownish fluid onto the hastily covered table on which it sat. The forensic team had also arrived together with Seth Riley, the Police Surgeon.

"So this is it, is it? The cause of panic, consternation and the collective twitching of the many members of the press now camping out in the restaurant?" Bob asked.

"That's it, spotted at 10.30 by Geoff, one of our cleaners. According to the label it came in on the early flight from

Gatwick. We checked the passenger list and we think the name's false."

"Oh. Why?" Bob asked, interested.

"The owner of said bag was allegedly called Mr Michel Souris. A rough translation being Mr Michael Mouse." Geoff huffed and scratched gently at an irritating, yellow-headed pustule on the side of his neck.

"Helpful," sighed Bob, trying not to look as the spot burst. "So, who gets to open it first?" he enquired.

At the words 'open' the crowd of bodies around the case thinned, to the point where only Bob, Seth, Dave and the youngest member of the forensic team remained.

Seth sighed and at a nod from Bob and Dave, began to carefully unzip the quietly dripping suitcase.

When opened it revealed a collection of damp clothing, two or three garishly coloured rolled socks and a large round object wrapped in a Marks and Spencer carrier bag. Gingerly, the plastic was removed to reveal a fast thawing severed head.

There was a collective intake of breath and then a quiet gagging noise, as the smell hit.

The eyes stared at them unblinkingly. Huge, brown, mucus-encrusted orbs. Matted and damp woolly curls clung limply to the large skull, whose twin horns of curved bone glimmered under the bright invasive lights.

"I think," Seth remarked reflectively, "my services may be superfluous but I can recommend a good vet."

There was an almost relieved intake of breath from everyone. The youngest member of the forensic team emitted a high, nervous titter.

"Make a nice bit of brawn from that," Dave observed. "Difficult to get a decent sized sheep's head nowadays."

Bob muttered blasphemously under his breath, as Seth carefully turned the head and his gloved hands removed a page of sodden paper wedged underneath an ear. Turning it towards the light he silently read the three printed words with a good deal of puzzlement.

REMEMBER THE TIDEMASTER

Bob leant against the case to get a better look and as he did, his eye caught sight of a brown parcel label tied with string to the elasticated belt inside the case. His heart sank as he read what the label said.

Please return to Sir Arthur Felton

Seth, Dave and he exchanged looks. Sir Arthur was one of the old school, ancient and still influential. What had been a possible prank was now looking increasingly ominous and even worse, political.

"Isn't his grandson our recently elected Euro MP?" Seth asked.

"Yes," Bob wearily replied. "The obnoxious little prat got in."

"Ah well, rather you than me, then," Seth remarked with a grin, as he repacked his bag and began to remove the plastic gloves from his hands.

***

Brian Clague fished around in his pockets for a cigarette – a futile attempt, tinged with no small amount of desperation. With appalling clarity he remembered the previous night. Champagne, golden bubbles tickling the sides of the fluted glasses, soft music (Ry Cooder and the Buena Vista Social Club). The mellow gleam of candlelight playing on the ring he'd placed, hands trembling, breath held, on the third finger of Caroline Howard's left hand.

"She'd said yes, she'd said Yes, she'd said YES!"

And he'd agreed to give up smoking.

There had, after all, to be a downside to everything.

Perhaps he ought to ring his Mum? Let her know the

good news. Or he could wait for a better moment ... or he could ring his Dad and his father could then ring her?

His parent's split, after twenty-five years of marriage, had brought out the cynic in his normally passive mother, shocking her children to the core.

Brian rubbed his eyes and sighed. The only thing marring the evening had been the sudden call-out over the mysterious bodysnatcher, and he'd only gone because poor old Harold was an old friend of his father's. One good thing about marrying an ex-copper was the tacit understanding that every moment had to be savoured, before the phone rang.

Not that it meant you didn't receive an ear bending; just that the person bending your ears knew that it wasn't your fault.

Brian sighed and wondered if he'd left a half-smoked packet in his desk – nothing. It was when he had the sudden idea to see if the cleaner had done the bins and had his head bent halfway into the metal rim, that he realised he was being watched.

"Had a bad night then, lad?" Bob Callow asked amusedly.

"I was just looking for something," Brian muttered, red in the face. "I thought you were on two weeks' leave, decorating and such like?" Brian straightened up and began to shuffle the papers on his desk.

"Couldn't keep away. Got any coffee? Because if you haven't I'd like my desk back," Bob stated.

"I was just ..."

"Never mind what you was just, justing. Yours is the little bit of plywood over there. The one with the large potted municipal triffid, the bad taste ashtray from Barnsley and the signed photo of Ben Elton."

Brian gathered up his belongings, including the shoes he'd kicked off under the desk and withdrew to his normal allotted space.

"They get more room in the cells," he grumbled.

"Want me to give old Harris a ring and see if they've got any vacancies?" Bob asked, his face a picture of studied innocence.

"No."

"Right, so anything happen while I was off?"

Brian managed to bite back a retort of, "But you still are off!" and expelled heavily before replying between carefully gritted teeth.

"Not much. We had a break in at the RAFA club. Mostly petty vandalism and they pinched a bit of booze, Clive has a hunch young Terry Q was the ringleader."

"Then it probably was. Pity we can't send him down the old lead mines."

"That's what Clive says, especially when you consider what will happen if we get him into court."

"Nothing."

"Exactly. We even have the video film of him and his mates slashing seats at the Gaiety! And what happened? The Gaiety manager got a right rollicking for making a citizen's arrest and Terry got a flea in his ear and a new social worker. Pity they can't send twelve-year-olds up chimneys."

"With hot coals under their feet. Yes, they were the days, eh Brian? The age of consent was thirteen and you could buy a little girl from her 'ever loving' parents for a fiver. Give her a nice phial of chloroform, take her to the nearest brothel and ensure she had a night to remember, eh?"

"Have you been reading again?"

"No, listening to Radio Four in the car park while Moira buys up Tescos. Speaking of which, how's young Caroline?"

"Fine, I mean, I asked her to …"

"And?"

"She said yes."

"Good, Moira can buy a hat, take her mind off that stippling she wanted done in the kitchen. Hang on a bit – you're not even considering buggering off to Barbados or Jamaica or whatever, are you?"

"Only for the honeymoon."

"Good. Let me know what you need for the new house and I'll sort something out."

"Actually you were the only one we argued over."

"Oh?" Bob looked up from the book he'd been rummaging through.

"Thing is Caroline would like you to give her away, her Dad being in Australia and ex-communicated and you did save her life last year ..."

"I did nothing more than reach her first, lad."

"And I'd like you to be best man."

"Two speeches, Moira will love that. Tell young Caroline I'd be delighted and if you don't have friends of your own age you're a sad man, young Brian."

"Oh!" Brian's face fell several notches and Bob, catching the look, relented.

"Don't see why I can't do both though. Ask the vicar, if he says yes I will and I'm not having anything to do with no registry office wedding. It's the church and old Roland giving you the third degree first off or nothing."

"Does he really try to put people off?"

"Oh aye. It's like a Gestapo interview without the lamps. As he says, marriage is for life not just until you decide to change the wallpaper. He's done enough work with juveniles to know that it's the kids who get the worst of the fallout. Young Luis and Bethany from next door but one have just split up and the youngest sprout can't be more than fourteen months. Mind you, it'll be nice to sit in the garden without listening to her threatening suicide and him mass murder."

"Bob?"

"Spit it out."

"Water feature for the garden, that's what you said you were doing. You took a whole two weeks off. Look it's there on the calendar, in writing!" Brian pointed to the wallchart neatly pinned to the wall above the spare desk. Bob regarded it with a thoughtful expression and groaned softly.

"Glass ball, surrounded by a miasma of multi¬coloured pebbles."

"What's a miasma when it's at home?"

"Dunno and now because she watched some gardening programme on Tuesday, it's a fully filtered lap pool with solar panels. Which is all very well but I'm going to have to take the back gate off its hinges and knock down half the wall to get the bloody digger in."

Brian shook his head to clear the vision of Bob sitting astride a JCB and hastened back to his original question.

"So if you're supposed to be up to the proverbials in do-it-yourself holes, why are you here?"

"Some sick puppy left a sheep's head in a suitcase at the airport. They thought it might be human and the boss dragged me away from lilac dado rails and passionfruit pink emulsion in time for my sight to return. I really do wish Moira would stop reading those infernal designer magazines. And before you ask that was the indoor job in case it rained."

"Sheep's head?"

"Frozen, wrapped in several carrier bags in a plain, scruffy, plastic suitcase. Security thought it was a real head, at first."

"Ah!" Brian, finally lost for words, sat at his desk with his mouth open.

"You look like a cod fish, lad," Bob observed, glancing at him.

"They must have a name of who it belonged to?"

"Oh, aye they did, not much help though unless ..."

"Unless what?"

"Unless there really is some poor sod whose warped parents decided to christen him Michael Mouse!"

"Ah. So you don't think that was his real name then?" Bob watched him for a few thoughtful seconds and sorrowfully shook his head.

"Either you haven't had much sleep lad or the thought of legal sex has addled the old grey cells," he observed.

Brian went a deeper shade of red and began to try to explain about Harold.

"It wasn't that. One of my father's old friends ..." His voice tailed off as Bob, plainly listening with only half an ear, finally found what he was looking for.

"Never do favours for relics, that's ... Ah – got him."

"Who?"

"Sir Arthur bleeding Felton."

"Who's he?"

"Only one of this blessed Island's first sons and the grandfather of our first Euro MP."

"Not pie-faced pooh breath?"

"Who?"

"It's what we called Ian Felton-Cholmondley at school."

"Forgot you went to that posh prison next to the airport."

"What does it say?"

"Read it yourself." Bob passed over the copy of Who's Who that he'd been searching through and thoughtfully tapped the relevant page.

The phone rang and Bob answered it, a worried frown appearing on his face as he tersely muttered, "Yes, I'll tell him."

Slowly he replaced the receiver, and looking Brian

straight in the eye, demanded sweetly, "That was Cora our friendly coastguard and she wants me to tell you she thinks she may have found your body. What body?"

"That was what I was trying to tell you!" Brian exclaimed indignantly, before hastily adding, "Great, she didn't say where then?"

"No, just that she'd meet you in her office in Peel."

"Right!"

"Where are you going?"

"Peel."

"Not without me, you're not."

"What about Sir Arthur?"

"We can see him afterwards, it's on the way back. Besides my nose is twitching at the very thought of your missing cadaver. You can drive."

Brian raised his eyes heavenwards and grabbing his jacket from the hook on the back of the door, reluctantly followed his superior from the room.

Slowly one of the shadows left behind when the fluorescent lights had been switched off and the door had been slammed shut, moved towards Bob's desk. The figure sat on Bob Callow's recently vacated chair and turned the book towards him. Thoughtfully he read the brief details of Sir Arthur's life, tapping the page when he'd finished. He knew there was something missing, something secret, which needed digging out before the killing could be stopped.

He just wasn't totally convinced that he wanted to reveal what it was.

A door banged, a gust of air blew Bob's office door inwards, dust scattered and the figure faded just as a young woman made to shut it again. She shook her head; for a moment she thought she'd seen a movement, a slight tremor at the edge of her vision.

With a shudder she shut the door and continued her

walk down the brightly lit corridor. Behind her the book fell to the floor and landed with a thump.

***

Sir Arthur Felton regarded his reflection in the mirror with the same intensity of expression that a truly vain woman half his age would. It would have to do. Bones ached and joints creaked as he fumbled with his tie. Dressing seemed to now take half a morning, whereas in the past he'd been known to dress in minutes before racing across cold frost-encrusted concrete to reach his waiting plane. In his head, old memories stirred. Vapour streaming wraithlike across the short grass runways. The shrill high-pitched sounds of sirens spun by hand. The shouts and curses of the engineers desperate to move the planes, stranded like clipped geese on runways and in hangars already strafed with bullets. Fired by an enemy invisible until that heart-numbing moment when they burst from the centre of a white-gold sun or from the blue-edged rims of dark grey clouds.

Carefully he pulled a navy blue V-necked sweater over his head and after brushing the few strands of hair still clinging to his balding pate, stood stiffly to attention and saluted his elderly reflection.

Limping slightly and aided by a silver-topped malacca cane, he moved towards the bedroom door and after waiting a few minutes to catch his breath, emerged quietly into the sun-filled hall.

Carefully he moved towards the library, its brown lacquered door propped open with an old elephant's foot umbrella stand. Sunlight moved within, warming the faded chairs and the dull, dappled patchwork carpet of elderly dragons and armoured warriors. Outside, beyond the French windows, dew sparkled on lush foliage and creamy petals. He could smell roses and in his imagination could almost feel their soft velvet heads teasing his skin with promises of sensual abandonment. He'd always liked roses, not as his daughter Constance believed because they were so typically English but because they reminded him of the gaily-clad prostitutes he'd frequently spent many happy hours with in Italy and France. He'd even – to the consternation and despair of his family – married one. 'Oh Estelle,' he murmured to himself, 'if only you and the boy had survived, perhaps things would have been different.'

He shrugged and moved towards his desk and the comfortable leather chair behind it.

Books filled the dark wood shelves covering every wall. Above the fireplace hung a large oil painting by some long-dead artist of repute. He could never remember the name or decipher the signature but the painting itself commanded the eye to move closer. Ships foundered, fiery furnaces of twisting metal, planes circling, diving to strafe the carrier and frigates below. Water boiled and just to the left the conning tower of an emerging submarine was barely visible between oil-flecked waves. Constance hated that picture, as did the remaining younger members of his immediate family.

Two green leather club chairs sat either side of the fireplace. In one lounged his old black labrador, Muskett. In the other a large elderly Persian cat washed itself in a patch of sunlight.

Sir Arthur lowered brittle bones into his chair and sat waiting. He loved this room. If he closed his eyes he could still see his father striding from window to fireplace and back as he pondered weighty judgments or the latest trial. Even now he could almost taste the aromatic smell of the pipe tobacco that always used to cloak his father's form, suspended in the dusty air.

Today he would begin to dissect his life and bare his soul to that young writer, an old friend of his daughter's.

Some things he'd keep hidden. After all they had happened a long time ago and the main protagonists were mostly dead or as good as. He shuddered and considered lighting the fire. An extravagance, he knew, but the one thing that could still keep his old bones and his thoughts warm.

A doorbell rang and the silence of the morning was dispelled with female voices and ready laughter. He straightened his shoulders and threw back his chin, ready and waiting. A woman entered and stood quietly in the doorway taking in the books and finally Sir Arthur himself. Their eyes met and held and Sir Arthur smiled. She was not what he'd imagined; taller, prettier and the eyes were sharp and far more intelligent than he'd been expecting.

"Where would you like to sit, my dear?" he asked, standing to attention, the old roué as always leaping to the fore.

"Oh anywhere would do. All you need to do is talk, I'll listen and then ask a few questions and when I have some sort of idea as to the eventual content of the book we'll start rummaging through the paperwork. If that's how you'd like to do it?" she added, moving in fascination to the picture over the mantelpiece.

"Do you like it?" he asked, watching her face as she drank in the details of the battle before her.

"I think 'like' is not the right word, but I can almost feel it."

"Yes, I know." Sir Arthur sighed and carefully lowered himself into one of the fireside chairs, dislodging the cat with the end of his walking stick. The cat, eyes yellow with spoilt malevolence, spat. The dog, watching from the other chair yawned, displaying a long pink tongue and drool-covered yellow teeth.

"I was there, you see. That plane, the one diving to the left of the cliffs, that's me." Sir Arthur raised his stick to illuminate his point, his entire face sharp with animation.

Tavistock, looking down, caught a glimpse of the man he'd once been and felt a sudden affinity.

"At least you survived," she remarked, turning back to the picture.

"Many didn't, my dear Mrs Allan, many didn't."

Sir Arthur, his mind's eye brimming with memories, blinked rapidly and then noisily blew his nose into a large blue-edged handkerchief. "Sentimental old fool," he thought.

Tavistock gave the painting a final long lingering look. She could almost hear the scream of the engines and the cries of men clinging to the floating flotsam. Waves splashed against the hull of the sinking vessel, an oily mix of green and brown and red.

Slowly she turned away from the large canvas and smiled at Sir Arthur. He smiled back, the spell suddenly broken.

"Right then, let's start shall we? You were born ..." Tavistock began.

Birds sang in the garden beyond the French windows, bees buzzed and hummed and somewhere the whirr of a lawnmower moved across the distant lawns.

Sir Arthur sat and listened and then stood up, reaching for his stick.

Tavistock, puzzled, looked on.

"I think," he said. "I'd like to do this in the garden under the trees. That is, if you don't mind. I have a sudden need for sunshine." He smiled at her. Blue eyes twinkled from beneath bushy white eyebrows.

"That's fine with me," Tavistock agreed, picking out a small tape recorder and her supply of tapes from within the cluttered contents of her canvas shoulder bag.

"Would you mind carrying some of those albums for me?" he asked her, pointing to a large cardboard box lounging on the floor beside his desk.

"The ones at the top are the most ancient. I thought

they would help to give you a better picture of the early years."

"Yes they would, thank you."

Ten minutes later they were settled in white-painted wicker chairs with mint green, pink and cream chintz cushions. Constance had appeared with a large silver tray of tea, coffee and delicate home-baked biscuits, almost as soon as Tavistock had brought out the last album. Sir Arthur thanked his daughter with genuine affection and asked her to stay. Constance declined – rather too hastily in Tavistock's silent view – and Sir Arthur watched his daughter move away, his face etched in sudden sadness. With a curious little movement of the head he seemed to almost pull his thoughts back and began to open the oldest of the sun-bleached family albums.

"My mother," he said, pointing to a sepia-toned print of a very beautiful young woman clad in a long trailing dress of silk, trimmed with beads and lace, her hair a glossy bob in the archetypal cut normally associated with the roaring twenties. Her eyes, kohl-rimmed and bright, smiled at the camera: an Edwardian Cleopatra.

"She's beautiful!" Tavistock remarked, fascinated by the photographs before her.

"Lady Elizabeth Gunner. And that handsome chap in the tennis whites is, or rather was, my father Sidney Felton."

"He looks fun!" Tavistock exclaimed, without really knowing why.

"He was!" Sir Arthur beamed at her. "Apparently he got sent down from Oxford for having young ladies in his room after the pumpkin hour; one of them was the then Under Secretary of State's granddaughter." Sir Arthur chuckled.

"There you are, that little chap in the Wee Willie Winkie outfit, that's me aged a couple of weeks."

"Oh, you're so cute! I really wish I had one of George

like that."

"Your son?"

"Yes."

"Ah. Any more?"

"Two girls, Kate and Emily. Ages nine and five respectively. George is seven going on seventy which is why a picture of him in an outfit like that would be worth its weight in gold by the time he reached puberty!"

Sir Arthur laughed outright, the skin around his eyes creasing in merriment.

"I rather think my mother did much the same thing when I brought my first girlfriend home for tea after we met at some dance or other. Now what was her name? I'll be blowed if I can remember it now and yet at the time ..."

They sat in pensive silence, each remembering their own first love. And then with an abrupt shake of his shoulders, Sir Arthur brought them both back into the present day.

"Ah well, youth eh? It never changes." Sir Arthur gave a small, self-deprecating cough and, eyes sparkling, took a sip of coffee before continuing.

"I was born April 14th 1921, the second of four children. My father was a mill owner by birth and an architect by choice, which is how he met my mother. She was the daughter of an eminent member of the consortium financing the building of docks and warehouses in Liverpool. My maternal grandfather did not approve of the match, having already chosen an eminent rising politician with influence and wealth as my mother's future husband. Mother, from what I can gather, hated her father's choice at first sight. He was, according to her, a brute. Whether she meant he was oafish and callous, as many politicians were at that time or simply physically violent, I have no idea. Her father tried to pack her off on a cruise but she managed to give her chaperone the slip during the embarkation festivities and then eloped with my father to Gretna Green which is why they both settled in the Island shortly afterwards. I believe their respective fathers hated each other on sight and my maternal grandfather would have met with more than strong disapproval if he'd had the temerity or indeed the courage to have stepped foot on Manx soil."

"Oh?" Tavistock asked, intrigued. "What did they – your paternal family – intend to do?"

"Something involving horsewhips and guns," Sir Arthur chuckled. "My grandfather was nothing if not forthright and extremely vocal when it came to my mother's father. He adored her, you see, and couldn't bear to think that anyone would deliberately want to make her unhappy."

Sir Arthur paused and took a sip of coffee. "My mother's mother, however, was all for the love match and presented my mother with a small package before she left on her cruise. The package contained a large and very valuable set of pearls, rubies and amethysts. Which had, I think, originally belonged to her mother, together with a beautiful lace christening rol . I believe that she also left strict instructions with various members of the crew to aid my mother in her escape – and possibly with the chaperone as well. But I'm afraid that it is probably merely supposition."

"A brave woman."

"Yes, I rather think she was. I don't believe, from what I could gather from my own mother, that her marriage was at all happy. She joined the suffragette movement and died a few years after my mother left, not that one led to the other."

"But?" Tavistock asked, sensing a story.

"I always got the impression that my maternal grandfather disapproved more because of her meeting people who he would consider not his sort than the politics of the thing. I remember an old aunt of mine, a positively poisonous old witch, saying that it was all to do with jealousy."

"Oh?" Tavistock prompted.

Sir Arthur lowered his voice and leant conspiratorially towards her. "She said that the man involved was a few years younger and a doctor. Apparently they were thinking of running away to America, he had an uncle with a large practice in Washington, or somewhere."

"Good grief!"

"Unfortunately she died before they could sort it all out."

"Pity."

"Yes I rather feel that it was. My mother did try to attend the funeral but my grandfather had her forcibly removed from the church."

"Good God!"

"To be perfectly honest, my parents both thought that my grandfather had had something to do with my grandmother's death, although what it was they never, to my knowledge found out. My father tried to get at the truth but was met by an official wall of red tape and the old boy network."

"What happened to your maternal grandfather after that?"

"He eventually died of syphilis and liver failure. I believe it was painful and long drawn out. My parents never spoke to him again, although he did write via his solicitor to ask to see my mother and her children before he died. He then left my mother his entire estate."

"Oh, did he repent do you think?"

"I don't think so, I believe he did it out of spite."

"Why?"

"Most of it was mortgaged to the hilt. The tenant farms had been run down to the point where none but the dregs of the farming community would consider working them. The rest of the estate was situated in South Africa, which was having its own problems at the time. The manager out there was corrupt and some sort of despot and therefore made the whole thing totally unmanageable from England, let alone the Isle of Man."

"What did your parents do?"

"My father went off to England to survey the mess and came back an older and wiser man. Basically they sold off the estate piece by piece by paying off the debts on one, improving the property and land and then selling it off as quickly as possible. The African property and farmland he sold at a knock-down price to one of his more adventurous friends who wanted to settle out there."

"Did this friend sack the manager?"

"Not exactly, he shot him." Sir Arthur finished the last of his coffee and smiled at Tavistock over the rim of the cup. "I rather believe he deserved it."

"Oh."

"Actually the ironic thing was that out of the entire estate the only portion worth anything was the South African land. One of the mines was found to contain a rich vein of diamonds and later became part of the De Beer empire. Unfortunately my father sold it off before that was discovered."

"Was this before or after the, er, shooting?"

"Who can tell? I have a postcard somewhere from his friend ... Ah here it is – took a while to get to my father. Apparently he was amused by it. Perhaps you can decipher it, my eyes are not as sharp as they used to be."

Tavistock picked up the yellowing piece of card and bent her head down to examine the writing. A frisson of something travelled from her fingertips to her brain and she only had time to think, "Oh God, not again," before the heat and the smell of human sweat assailed her senses.

Against a grey, roughly plastered wall crouched a human form. Perspiration lay white and glistening on chocolate brown skin and a trickle of blood ran from nose to chest. The white cotton blouse was torn, the dark skirt ripped from ankle to thigh. Breasts rose and fell and deep red scratches glowed against the soft oiled skin. The girl, barely a woman, took in deep gulps of air and pushed herself towards the door and the beckoning light with shaking limbs. In front of her a man crawled towards the polished boots of another.

His face was pockmarked with deep pits and running sores. He was shouting in the shrill drawl of the Afrikaner.

"For Christ's sake speak English," spat the voice belonging to the boots.

"She's a kaffer, she's nothing. Why bother? If I don't have her someone else will."

"She's only ten for God's sake. Christ, I have a ten-year-old sister at home."

"You want her yourself Meester? You take her, plenty more where that came from." The crawler replied, his voice suddenly sly.

"I don't want her," came the reply, the disgust in the voice only barely concealed.

"Then let me finish what I've started, you can watch if you want. I like 'em young or old, makes no difference."

"Ever had them older. I mean a lot older?" A separate voice asked.

"Don't know what you're getting at." The man rose slowly to his feet. Polished boots moved back.

"I mean, I heard you'd slept with something a bit more upper class. Though frankly I can't say I believed it. I mean, would any woman of breeding let you take her? I expect they'd rather not." The voice drawled and spat on the ground, an inch away from the Afrikaner's feet.

"For your information I have and she begged for more. Begged, I tell you."

"A poor widow then."

"Much you know – her husband paid me to take her, teach her a lesson. Feisty enough at the start I grant you. Look."

Slowly he pulled up the tail of his shirt and half turned. A purple scar glowed against the sunburnt skin. Long and jagged, still wrinkled and red in the centre.

"If she did that to you, she couldn't have enjoyed it that much." Polished boots remarked.

"Maybe not at the beginning but she stopped struggling later on, when she realised her loving husband wasn't going to stop me."

"What!"

"He paid me and then he watched. Even helped me tie her down. He was particular about the knots. Didn't want to leave any marks. Pity she died."

"You murdered her!" Polished boots shouted. Something raced the air and then the leather of the whip connected to the Afrikaner's cheek. Skin ripped and tore, exposing white bone.

"No, no. She bled and there was an infection or something. She died after I'd gone, days afterwards. It wasn't my fault. How was I to know she was pregnant? Besides he said it wasn't his, couldn't have been. That's why he did it."

"Who?"

"Lord Gunner. Listen to me, English, if the nobs can prostitute their own wives I can take this blackie; besides she's mine. I bought her, fair and square. Paid as good a price as you would in London. If her parents are happy with the arrangement, I don't see why you shouldn't be. Besides, it's none of your business."

"Her parents only agreed because you refuse to let them work if they don't. They know as well as you do that they have no choice," polished boots pointed out, his voice sharp with anger. He turned to his companion, still half hidden amongst the shadows and fingered the butt of his whip, a look of enquiry on his face and barely suppressed violence in his eyes.

"Shoot him. I've all I need to satisfy the new owner," came the cold reply to his unspoken question. The Englishman moved further back into the shadows and the Afrikaner, unbelievingly and realising too late that this time there would be no opportunity to negotiate, tried to stand.

The sound of a single shot reverberated around the walls. A red flower bloomed and blossomed within the Afrikaner's head. The body collapsed slowly onto the dusty floor. Dark hands moved towards the girl and carried her gently out of sight. There were muttered thanks as muted wisps of cordite moved slowly upwards.

"Throw him in the river with the other rubbish and let the alligators feed. Then we clear out the old guard and I shall write and let Sidney know," the Englishman ordered, holding a delicate linen handkerchief to his nose to keep out the stench of blood now permeating the air around him.

Motes of dust mingled with the heat and light in front of Tavistock's eyes, the sounds of footsteps and that of a body being dragged across the dried mud floor faded.

"Are you all right, my dear?" Sir Arthur leant towards Tavistock. Tavistock looked up and returned his worried gaze. Sweat beaded on her skin, white against a summer tan.

"Yes, I sometimes, sometimes, have too vivid an imagination. I'm all right now."

"So what does it say?" Constance asked. She'd arrived quietly with fresh lemonade and had noted her friend's silence and staring eyes with concern. The card still clutched in Tavistock's hand was one she had never until that day seen before.

"It says, 'Vermin extermination now completed. Rumours confirmed at source as discussed at Langharn.

She may RIP. You owe me a bottle of best Krug. Regards H.'"

"Who's she?" Constance asked, intrigued.

"Father never said. When I asked he said it was code for the company striking rich and being worth a sell-out. I always assumed they'd somehow paid off the old manager, turned the company around and sold it off at a profit when they hit the new diamond vein or whatever they call it."

Tavistock, the feeling of nausea that had hit her passing as quickly as it had come, tried to smile and gratefully accepted a glass of lemonade, the glass blessedly cold to the touch.

"I think I'll finish there, for now, if you don't mind," she declared, taking a gulp of the sharply sweet citrus drink.

"No, of course not," Sir Arthur agreed, giving her a kindly yet puzzled look. "Spot of lunch out here. What do you say?"

"Well ..." Tavistock turned towards Constance.

"Please do," Constance smiled back, her face suddenly youthful as the skin lifted and the eyes sparkled back. "We always lunch out here during the summer and you can give me all the gossip from your last trip. It can be a mite boring, just Father and I."

"Fine. I'd be delighted." Tavistock sat back and smiled at them both, washing the images of an Africa long ago from her inner eye.

"Before we finish, though ..." Tavistock began, after Constance had moved back towards the house and her waiting kitchen.

"Yes?"

"What happened to your parents?"

"My father's parents both died within days of each other, shortly before my father's return to the Island and being the only child he took over the running of the mills and farms that the family then owned. In retrospect he took on more than he'd expected and because of the legal aspect to a lot of his business, became interested in the law. He qualified late in life but still managed to become Attorney General and then Deemster. My mother, bless her, became a magistrate and I can remember some quite startlingly good arguments across the dinning table, before and after I left for Oxford."

"They were happy?"

"Oh yes, very. The only regret my mother ever mentioned was her having to leave her own mother. But then again that's part and parcel of growing up. Don't you think?"

"Oh, yes I suppose it is." Tavistock sat back and then after a brief pause asked. "You said you had three other siblings, what happened to them?"

"My older brother Charles died during the war, he was trying to rescue a family from their house during the Blitz and it fell in on him. Letty or Letitia as she was christened, married an Australian and they have a vineyard out there. Make a very good living out of it too, by all accounts. Charlotte, the baby of the family, died from scarlet fever when she was barely ten."

Tavistock searched for something to say and while she was still floundering, Constance emerged from the shadow of the house, pushing a small wooden trolley with squeaky wheels.

"I know I'm just like that poor long-suffering butler in 'The Importance of being Earnest'," she stated, breaking the silence.

"No tea and cake then?" Tavistock laughed, suddenly warm again.

"No, just a chicken salad and ice-cold Ozzy Chardonnay."

Sir Arthur smiled at them both and sat back as the lightly

golden wine was poured into his glass.

***

Bob and Brian sat behind the computer screen in mute fascination. Cora clicked the mouse and sat back in her seat.

"There you go then, it's perfectly feasible that if a body was dumped at Garwick it could end up at Port Moar early the following morning."

Bob had watched as the white dot and its accompanying cross spun with the computer-generated tide, until finally it came to rest, almost exactly where the early morning coastguard patrol had found a body washed up at Garwick, at half past seven that morning.

"You were lucky, if this is the man that was seen being dragged into the sea late yesterday evening, and according to the computer there's a good probability that it is. The fact that your attacker was disturbed could have meant that he didn't drag him far enough out."

"Oh?" Brian asked enquiringly.

"Watch. For instance, if the body was dragged out past the rocks and the wind had freshened from a five to say a seven and changed direction to a south-westerly."

Bob and Brian watched as the dot spun out to sea.

"Scotland," Brian muttered.

"Exactly, and heaven alone knows what condition it would have been in," Bob mused, frowning down at the gently glowing console in front of him.

"Anything else?" Cora asked as she exited the programme before turning off the screen. "Because I've got a training exercise to run in twenty minutes."

"Nope, that's been very useful." Bob smiled and stretched, before rising and moving over to the window through which the sounds of gulls and the putter of boat engines could be heard. The view was of sky, cliffs, the harbour and Peel Castle, its ragged remains looming over the fishing boats and trawlers tied to its grey stone skirts.

Bob sniffed loudly, taking in the mixed and pungent aroma of kipper and mud flat scented air. 'Still,' he thought to himself, 'anything has got to be better than being at home surrounded by the innards of water pumps and a motley assortment of little screws and woody bits I've absolutely no bloody idea what to do with.'

"Come on Brian lad, every cloud has a silver lining somewhere," he said aloud.

Cora and Brian exchanged perplexed expressions, as Bob shrugged himself back into his grey fleece jacket. Brian, used to Bob's at times erratic trains of thought, trawled back through his memory to find anything which could even be remotely considered good news and gave up after the first thirty seconds.

Bob and Brian thanked Cora profusely and then trudged back down the wooden stairs to the front door. Outside, the smell of seaweed, mud and the smoky aroma of curing fish assailed their senses. Bob drew in deep breaths and headed not to their waiting car, but to the Peveril public house across the road.

"Lunch," Bob barked as he negotiated a path littered with urns and pots brimming with multi-coloured foliage and large bright pink geraniums.

"Isn't it a bit early for that?" Brian asked, checking his watch.

"It's never too late for a couple of kippers, lime marmalade and some brown bread and butter." Bob opened the large, darkly stained double doors and sailed inside. Brian paused momentarily before following in his wake. For all of his size he felt like a small tug caught in the slipstream of a supertanker.

Inside, Bob was already chatting to the landlady and

ordering two plates of kippers and a pot of tea for two.

Later they sat in solitary silence in the back room, Bob picking the remaining fishbones from his teeth with a cocktail stick and Brian trying not to notice.

"Now that really hit the spot, don't you think?" Bob asked between stabs. "Ah – got the bugger!" Joyfully he deposited the bone and now soggy stick in the ashtray.

"Bob?"

"What?"

"Do you think he was disturbed?"

"Who?"

"The murderer."

"Dressing up as a long lost brother of 'The Thing from the Black Lagoon' and drowning people, of course he's disturbed; proper basket case." Bob found the chewing gum he was searching for in his pocket. Carefully, he unwrapped one stick and popped it in his mouth. "Want some?" he asked, heavy jowls masticating in a fair imitation of the local sheep.

"No. I meant, do you think that because Harold disturbed him he didn't drag the body out as far as he'd wanted to?"

"Meaning that it should be wending its merry way to the home of the wee dram and the Happy Haggis?"

"Yes."

"Possibly."

"That's what I thought."

"But we will probably never know, unless we catch the little bugger, with enough evidence to prove it. Now I have to go see a man about a sheep."

"Sir Arthur Felton?"

"The very same. You never know, perhaps my sheep is something to do with your body? Stranger things have happened."

Brian gave him an oddly piercing look but said

nothing.

Stranger things had happened the previous year and he hoped to the bottom of his soul that Bob was wrong.

"Why the long face? I was joking!" Bob enquired, piling the plates up before leaving them on the bar.

Brian tried to smile, failed and moved off.

Later as they drove to Sir Arthur Felton's manorial pile, with the sun shining and Manx Radio blurbing away in the background, the mental cloud surrounding Brian cleared, and as he drove past the wrought iron gates and up to the Georgian front door, he felt almost cheerful.

Chapter 6

July 8th p.m.

They were just finishing off the chicken salad when the doorbell rang. Tavistock looked up and met Sir Arthur's eyes.

"What was that?" Tavistock asked, as sounds not unlike her old school bell reverberated around the garden.

"Doorbell – had one of those electric bells installed outside the kitchen door," Sir Arthur chuckled, "which means that no one can creep up on me with the comment 'I rang the bell but no one heard so I thought I'd try to find you.'"

"Do people do that?" Tavistock asked, slightly shocked.

"Reporters do!" Constance replied. "Although I can't imagine who it could be at this time of day. Are you expecting anyone Father?"

"No."

"Perhaps it's a double glazing salesman," Tavistock said.

"If it is, I shall set the dog on them," Sir Arthur stated firmly. The dog, now lying at his feet in the hope that a piece of chicken would land within licking distance, yawned, stretched and rolled over onto its back.

They were still laughing when Bob and Brian, tired of

waiting, rounded the side of the house and suddenly spying their quarry, hurriedly marched towards them.

Bob grinned broadly at Tavistock's stunned expression.

"Well," he said, eyeing the plates. "Fancy meeting you in a place like this."

"You know this gentleman?" Sir Arthur asked, torn between amusement at Tavistock's obvious consternation and a sharp desire for the rest of his lunch.

"Er, yes. Sir Arthur, this is Detective Inspector Bob Callow and this is Detective Constable Brian Clague. Bob, Brian, may I introduce you to Sir Arthur Felton and his daughter Constance?"

"Pleased to meet you. I see I've interrupted your lunch," Bob observed, happily stating the obvious.

"Yes, can't this wait?" Constance asked, plainly irritated. She broke off as she caught the sudden look of abject longing on Bob's face, as he beheld the pudding, which was a splendid heap of sponge, strawberries and thick curls of yellow cream.

"Er, would you like something to eat Inspector? Or a cup or tea or coffee?" Constance added, slightly mollified.

Bob smiled and settled his bulk into the nearest vacant chair.

"Coffee would be very nice and maybe a small slice of that delicious looking dessert."

"I thought," Tavistock muttered, staring at him, "that you were supposed to be having a week or so off."

"Ah, well I was but when duty calls ..." Bob tailed off, avoiding eye contact with either Brian or Tavistock, both of whom were now openly glaring at him. Sir Arthur looked from one to the other and, smiling broadly, began to cut the cake whilst his daughter collected the now empty salad plates.

"Duty, Inspector?" he asked as he handed Bob a small delicate round of porcelain piled high with sugar-dusted strawberries and cream.

"Er, yes, perhaps we could discuss it a bit later, wouldn't want to put anyone off their dessert."

"I doubt very much whether you could but I appreciate the consideration," Sir Arthur stated, handing Bob an ornate silver fork and spoon.

"The thing is we, er … were called in to the airport this morning because someone had left a sheep's head in a suitcase and unfortunately it also contained a message and a label addressed to you, Sir Arthur."

Bob took a mouthful of cake and sighed with pleasure, as he appeared to deliberately ignore the effect he'd created. Three pairs of eyes watched in silence as Bob ate, carefully masticating each mouthful, whilst Brian surreptitiously watched Sir Arthur for any reaction.

"The message was 'Remember the Tidemaster.' And the label said 'Please return to Sir Arthur Felton.'"

A plate slipped from Constance's fingers and crashed to the ground. The noise created an explosion of vibrating sound, which was followed by a brief shocked silence.

"Constance?" Sir Arthur and Tavistock asked in unison. Bob looked from one to the other and held his peace.

"I'm all right, I'm fine. I'll just clear this up – I'll get a dustpan." Constance hurried off, clutching broken pieces of china in both hands, oblivious to the cuts they were making to her hands, blood oozing silently from her skin onto the translucent white shards.

She returned moments later, her hands wrapped in a blue striped linen tea towel, one of which held a stained plain brown envelope which she quietly handed to Bob.

Bob carefully placed the envelope on the table and sat back in his chair.

"And this is what exactly?" he asked.

"A letter addressed to me, a few newspaper cuttings and several photocopied sheets of a notebook," Constance replied.

"Do you mind if we ...?" Bob asked as Brian left his seat and went to stand behind him.

"No, please. To be honest it's a relief to show someone." Sir Arthur made a very slight movement and Constance, guiltily concerned, gently patted his hand.

Bob carefully donned a pair of light plastic gloves which Brian had quietly handed to him and with a definite feeling of déjà vu, extracted variously sized pages of coloured paper from the confines of the envelope.

"And how was this delivered exactly?" he asked, noting that the envelope displayed nothing that could even be remotely considered as a postmark.

"I don't honestly know," Constance replied, her lips pursed in concentration. "It was on the hall table with a collection of letters." She looked at him and frowned, forming the words in her head first before continuing. 'The whole thing has been odd,' she thought to herself. 'Almost like something out of one of father's beloved Sherlock Homes stories.'

"Letters?" Bob prompted.

"Yes, I always leave the letters to go out on the hall table, that was amongst them. I don't know how it got there. I asked around at the time. At first I thought it was a joke. That is, until I read it through."

"Surely not that many people wander through your house?" Bob asked.

"Well normally no, but on that particular day we had the gardens open for charity. You know the usual thing; we serve coffee and biscuits on the lawn for a small sum. Tavistock, you were here that day." Bob looked to Tavistock for reassurance. Tavistock frowned in concentration.

"When was that?" she asked.

"The twenty-fifth of June, we were raising money for the hospice, you must remember. Chloe Barnsworth's wretched child fell in the pond."

"Oh good grief, that coffee morning. Sorry Bob, I'm certainly not going to be much help to you, there were people all over the place."

"Ah, that morning. Found one of the blighters in my study! Threw him out pretty smartish." Sir Arthur mused darkly, scowling in remembrance. "Him and his blasted dog!"

Bob frowned. "So anyone could have come in, dropped it on the table and there is a cast of thousands available for the role of prime suspect?" Constance nodded in agreement and Bob frowned gloomily.

Bob bent back to the papers in his hand and carefully read the first thin blue sheet.

He looked up long enough to scowl at Brian and then read the letter again, just to make sure that he'd really read what he thought he had.

"Blackmail?" Bob asked, turning to the browned newspaper clippings and the photocopied pages of rough-looking notes. Sir Arthur, startled, glared at his daughter.

"Blackmail! Connie, why didn't you tell me?"

Constance shrugged; now that it was finally out in the open the feeling of relief was almost overwhelming. She blinked back a solitary tear.

"I thought about it but you were tired and you'd only just recovered from that awful bout of flu. I thought I could handle it."

"How?" Bob asked.

"By simply ignoring it."

"I see. So you didn't arrange a meeting?"

"No."

"Did you show this to anyone else?"

"My son."

"Ian!" Sir Arthur spluttered. Constance nodded and Tavistock, now beginning to enjoy herself, sat back and waited for the next development. She had already come to the conclusion that Sir Arthur had little love for his grandson. Her suspicions were confirmed as Sir Arthur pushed his daughter's hand from him and groped for his stick.

"That useless idiot. What did you go to him for? I'm your father for God's sake, I could have helped – and I tell you one thing Inspector, I would have come straight to you. What this son of a bitch needs is locking up! Constance how could you? You couldn't possibly have believed what ever lies he tried to tell you."

"I didn't know. You were ill and if anyone was to be affected it would have been Ian. So I asked him."

"That boy has lied since he was in short pants. The only consolation is that the government pays him to lie nowadays so I don't have to. Well what did the useless layabout advise?"

"He told me to ignore it."

"Good grief, the lad had a grain of sense! I bet he had to ask someone first though," Sir Arthur muttered maliciously.

"No, he didn't," Constance retorted. "He said that the press had been saying far worse things about him for years and that his sainted grandfather couldn't possibly have done anything treasonous."

"Oh? Please do repeat the rest of what he said. If you dare!" Her father folded his arms across his chest and waited.

"I, er ..." Constance looked from her father to the police and back again. There was a very pregnant silence. "He said that he couldn't imagine that it was true as you would never have been stupid enough to leave any evidence or, or ..." Her voice faltered.

"Go on."

"Or witnesses."

"I see."

"I'm sorry Daddy. You must understand you never speak about what happened during the war. I wondered if some of it might have been true and that somehow someone had may be got the wrong end of the stick. That's why I was so keen on you writing your memoirs, I thought …"

"That it would all come out in the wash. So to speak?"

"Yes."

"And would you mind letting me know just what it was that I was supposed to have done?"

"You killed a young man, knifed him to death and …"

"I was in Intelligence, of course I killed people and with knives. It was quieter than using a gun."

Bob chuckled and Sir Arthur, his gallows sense of humour returning, smiled. "Connie, before you were born, before I married your mother, I worked in France as a spy. I married a young woman and we had a child, a little boy." Constance, clearly stunned, sat up ramrod straight.

"What?" she hissed, hardly believing what she was hearing.

"They died in an explosion. I went a little mad and killed a lot of people. It was wartime and that's what you do. You kill or you get killed. I travelled about setting up groups of resistance fighters. Cells we called them. The Gestapo found out and they asked me a few rather impertinent questions. Luckily the place I was being held in was bombed before they could revive me enough from their first rather crude interview. I escaped and after reaching England was sent back here to, er, recover from my wartime experiences and to run an operation designed to find somebody we termed 'the Tidemaster'."

"And did you find him?" Bob asked, interested.

"Him or her, Inspector; many of Hitler's better agents were in actual fact women. No we didn't, but I came close. The records will state that we did and that he was killed in a riot but …"

"You don't believe it?"

"No, no I don't. It was all too neat, too tidy, too much like a stage set. I have always believed he came to the Island to make contact with someone and that when it failed, he or she managed to make their way to South America. Possibly from Ireland. I don't suppose it matters now but I always wondered why."

"Why?"

"Why the Isle of Man."

"Didn't we have that secret radar station up at Port Erin?" Brian asked. They all looked at him. "My granddad used to deliver bread up there. He told me that it was so secret he had to leave the loaves with the bloke on sentry duty, even though he'd known them for years. He always sounded a bit put out by it," Brian observed.

"Yes we did, but I don't believe this particular agent was interested in that. I always suspected he was more interested in propaganda."

"Doesn't sound too dangerous then," Constance remarked. Her father watched her for a brief moment, a thoughtful expression on his face.

"There was a very strong fascist movement during the thirties and Britain had more than its fair share of converts. When we finally went to war with Hitler it went underground. Did a lot of damage. Wars are run as much on information as on men.

"The Tidemaster travelled, setting up small groups of believers who wanted Hitler to win. He or she started in France and Poland before the occupation and then came to England after a stint in the Netherlands. The damage that was done to our intelligence services, and the lives that were lost due to the workings of those groups are probably incalculable. So when we believed that the Tidemaster had landed on the Isle of Man, I was sent to hunt him or her down and then to destroy any cells that may have been set up. I never did, despite what the records show."

"I'm sorry." Constance hung her head; relief, guilt and shame vying for attention.

"I know. You did what you thought was right as we all do."

"So you never met the blackmailer then?" Brian asked.

"I told you before. No I didn't," Constance replied, clearly ruffled.

"Did you receive anything else?" Bob enquired, his tone that of an avuncular uncle, whilst his glance at Brian was nothing if not threatening.

"No. I waited but nothing happened and I pushed it to one side. Until today."

"You could have come to us," Brian stated, deliberately ignoring his superior.

"And you would have done what exactly?" Sir Arthur asked mildly. Brian coloured and after catching Bob's eye retreated back into his notebook.

"Unless it had something to do with some kind of criminal act, probably not a lot," Bob reluctantly admitted.

"Do you mind if I hold on to these and let forensic have a look?"

"By all means be my guest," Sir Arthur replied. "And if you need any more information please don't hesitate to come back and ask."

"Thank you. I will."

Bob and Brian stood up and waving aside Constance's offer of seeing them out, made their way back to the drive and their waiting car.

"Why would we need to see him again?" Brian asked as he started the engine.

"Because he knows as I do that blackmailers rarely apply their trade to just one person."

"Oh?"

"For some reason this guy, and I tend to think it was a he, didn't make the next contact. Now why do you think that was?"

"Dunno, but I expect I'm about to learn," Brian muttered, turning the wheel and executing a ragged three-point turn in the drive. He missed an ancient tree stump and a large rock by mere inches as Bob pointedly wiped imaginary sweat from his brow.

"This advanced driving course you went on, did you pass? As I was saying, before fear temporarily deprived me of speech, either our blackmailer found someone else more willing and able to pay up or ..."

"Or what?"

"There's only one good thing about a blackmailer and that's a dead blackmailer."

"You think?"

"We have an unknown body in the morgue, who our one and only witness believes was waiting for someone. So either they could have been another victim or the blackmailer. It's going to be interesting to see if there are any fingerprints on our new piece of evidence and if any match our corpse."

"Don't you think it's stretching things a bit Bob? Could be coincidence."

"This is a small island lad, everyone knows everything about everyone else, so when was the last time we had a blackmailer?"

"Um ..."

"Exactly. Poison pen letters in abundance. Nasty rounds of gossip far more deadly than real bullets but deliberately drowned bodies, dead sheep and extortion? Forgive me lad, but I don't believe in coincidence and neither do you. I believe in my guts, young Brian."

"And what are they saying then?" Brian asked, grinning.

"That I've had too much cream," Bob replied, rubbing his gently churning stomach.

***

That evening Tavistock had other things to think about, in particular the renewed belief by her youngest that her Indian daddy had returned to live in the wardrobe. Tavistock surveyed the scene of chaos and carnage that was her daughter's bedroom and gritted her teeth. Somewhere under the assortment of Barbies, plastic kitchen utensils, Lego, clothes and books, was a pink carpet. Toy boxes lay on their sides like beached mammals, their brightly coloured guts spilling onto the floor as if a whirlwind had just passed.

"Clear this up now!" she shouted, hands on hips, lips pursed and eyes glittering. Emily squared up to her with two fingers firmly thrust in her mouth and shook her head.

"Do it now, or you get no pudding for tea." Again the defiant shake.

The fingers were removed long enough to shout. "It wasn't me!" and were then thrust back in.

"Oh. Who was it then'?" Tavistock shouted back.

"My Indian daddy."

Tavistock regarded her smallest child with utter exasperation. It had been a long day and she really didn't need this.

"Right, well you and your Indian daddy can tidy it all up before your ordinary daddy gets home and throws a major wobble or there will be no party on Saturday!"

"But Mummy ..." Emily wailed.

"No buts!" Tavistock stormed from the room and down the stairs, watched by George and Kate from the safety of doors open just far enough for them to know that their little sister was getting it in the neck. The news was greeted by both with the same level of guilty delight.

They heard Emily's shout of "I hate you Mummy!" followed by the sound of toys being thrown loudly back into their coloured receptacles.

Tavistock shut the kitchen door and leant against it, exhaled deeply and started counting to ten.

"She's only five you know," Mannanan remonstrated, solidifying gently in front of her.

"Keep out of this – she has got to learn to look after her things," Tavistock muttered, sinking into a kitchen chair and hiding her head in her hands.

"What if she behaves like that at school?"

"But she doesn't."

Tavistock looked up and fixed him with a chilly stare.

"Listen, when I want advice from a two-thousand-year-old spook, I'll ask for it. Just at the moment Emily has enough to cope with at school without telling fibs about some imaginative friend!"

"Er, about Emily's little friend; I really think there is something you should know."

"Why do I have the distinct feeling that today is about to get a lot worse?" Tavistock asked despairingly.

"Well, um, Emily's Indian daddy is me."

"What!" Tavistock sat up, stunned.

"She was lonely and needed someone to play with, so I play with her."

"Play with her?" Tavistock stared at him incredulously.

Find things and cook and er ..." Mannanan's voice tailed off as Tavistock slumped further into her chair and groaned.

"She can't see me, but she can hear me and I like her, she reminds me of someone."

"Who?" Tavistock asked suspiciously.

Mannanan sighed and sat down beside her.

"My daughter." The words were spoken softly but the pain of loss lay heavy in the air between them.

"I'm sorry, I didn't know that you had any children."

"Only one, Elaine's child. I left before she was born and was allowed no contact. I had to watch her grow, suffer, laugh, and die. Always at a distance, always terrified that I would make things worse."

"Ah." Tavistock, finally lost for words, reached out across the space between them and briefly touched his hand.

"Play with Emily by all means, but please tell her it's only a game, and only a home game at that."

"Oh she already knows that, my dear."

Tavistock looked at him. Behind them a door opened and a small grubby hand reached out and gently touched Tavistock's shoulder.

"I'm sorry Mummy."

Tavistock turned and bundled the small form onto her lap. Kissing the top of her head and brushing away the tears still gleaming on Emily's cheeks, she murmured softly in a small pink ear. "It's all right sweet pea. Your Indian daddy owned up and told me he did do it."

"Will he get no pudding?" Emily asked.

"Probably, unless he helps you tidy your room," Tavistock replied. "And I'm sorry I thought you were telling me fibs."

Emily, suddenly all smiles, pushed her mother away and ran to the door.

"And I don't hate you really, Mummy."

"Good, now go tidy your room and tell George and Kate that Daddy's bringing home fish and chips for tea."

After Emily had made her usual noisy exit, Mannanan quietly asked. "So, why exactly have you been in such a foul mood since your return from the Felton mansion?"

"What? I'm sure I don't know what you mean, I'm

just having a bad day, that's all." There was a thought-filled pause and Tavistock, refusing to make eye contact, could almost hear the word 'liar' reverberating around the room.

"Emily's room was a lot worse yesterday and you hardly noticed. Today you come home, throw the shopping around and castigate your children about everything under the sun. You even picked a fight with poor Richard and all he'd done was phone to let you know that he'd be late home."

"He's always late," Tavistock protested, flicking an assortment of breakfast crumbs from the table with the back of her hand.

"He isn't and you're lucky he lets you know when he is, a lot of husbands wouldn't."

"Have you finished?" Tavistock asked, stung.

"For the moment."

"Good."

"Well?"

"Nothing, it's nothing. I just need five minutes peace and the paper."

Mannanan stood up and moved closer. "You, young woman, are upset and I want to know why before blood is spilt."

"It's ..." Tavistock tried to find the right words, failed and bit her lower lip, in a frown of concentration. Mannanan stood with arms folded and waited.

"I have to lay the table," Tavistock mumbled, rising. Mannanan glared at her. "It can wait."

"Oh."

"And so can I, I'm a past master at waiting, I can wait for ever if necessary."

"Oh, all right." Tavistock looked at him and sighed. "The thing is, I saw something at the Feltons."

"Oh?"

"An attempted rape and then a fairly nasty murder. Not present day – ancient stuff, Victorian probably. Real, common or garden ancient bloodshed. From an old postcard of all things and …"

"Go on."

"Why me? Why do I get to see all the bad bits, why can't I, just for once, see someone enjoying life – a wedding or a party, anything? Last year was bad enough but it at least had a point, we were trying to track down a murderer, but this? All I was doing was looking through old letters in order to write an ancient warhorse's memoirs. That's all. I'm fed up with seeing death and horror. I really thought that after last year, it was all finished."

"In what way?"

"I've always seen bits of the past and snatches of the future, but it's all been hazy up to now. Now it's like I'm there and I really, really, thought it had all ended."

"You haven't seen anything like this before today?"

"No, not since the death of Juan Moss last year."

"And how do you feel?"

"I feel … cheated." Tavistock looked into eyes full of concern and burst into tears.

"And this is the first thing you've seen since then."

"Yes."

"Ah."

"Do you know why?" Tavistock, not receiving an answer, gave him a deeply suspicious look. "You do, don't you!" she fired back at him as she angrily rubbed her reddening eyes with her knuckles.

"I think someone is trying to find something and he or she is prepared to stop at nothing until they succeed."

"And this has something to do with the Feltons?"

"Yes."

"What?" Curiosity having dried up her tear ducts, Tavistock wiped her nose with the edge of her sleeve and

Mannanan, seeing her growing visibly calmer, sat down again. Resting his head in his hands, elbows digging into the varnished pine he stared at the dark woody grain in a thoughtful fashion. He would, he knew, have to be extremely careful how he handled the rest of the conversation.

"That's just it, I don't really know." Underneath the table he crossed his ankles.

"But you must."

"What do you think I am, omnipotent?" he said, feigning anger.

"Well …"

"Well I'm not. I just have this uneasy feeling of wrongness and your gift returning again is proof of that."

"Gift? Huh," Tavistock muttered.

"Yes a gift, a power given to you to help prevent something even worse happening. You only see the past, it can't be changed and it can't hurt you … but the future …"

"Could?"

"Yes."

"I hadn't thought of it that way before."

They sat with their individual thoughts in a companionable silence broken by the insistent ringing of the phone.

Kate ran in, clutching the portable telephone.

"It's Daddy, he'll be home in twenty minutes and he's bringing fish and chips and he'd like you to open a bottle of falling down juice." Kate deposited the phone in Tavistock's lap and hugged her. Tavistock picked it up and after listening for a minute or so muttered "Me too," and switched it off.

"Who wants to lay the table and get extra chips?" she called out, hearing the twin thumps of George walking and Emily jumping down the stairs.

"Me!" her offspring cried as they invaded the formerly

quiet kitchen and raced to the various cupboards for plates, mats and assorted cutlery.

Tavistock looked over their heads at Mannanan who grinned broadly and faded like the Cheshire Cat, his smile remaining until the last.

***

Bob Callow wallowed happily, naked amongst the steam and translucent green bubbles of the large American-style bath Moira had had installed before Christmas.

"You look ..." said a voice, "like a middle-aged hippo!"

Bob erupted from the water and glared angrily around.

"What ...?" he spluttered as he searched the bathroom for signs of life. Slowly the figure of Mannanan shimmered into view. Bob was not impressed.

"Is nowhere sacred?" he spat, regarding Mannanan from eyes which were about as far from showing the milk of human kindness as is possible without the hands actually waving a blunt instrument. "And will you leave the cacti alone!" he added.

Mannanan, who was gently prodding a particularly vicious-looking spiky succulent with a luridly opulent bright orange and purple flower sprouting from its side, stopped, gave Bob a sideways look and then after carefully replacing the toilet seat and lid, sat and silently surveyed him with a thoughtful expression.

"What?" Bob asked testily.

"Nothing really, just wanted a chat."

"A chat?"

"Exactly."

"Why am I getting the distinct impression that you have something on your mind but you don't think I'm going to take it at all well?" Bob asked reaching for a plastic submarine from the side of the bath. Mannanan pursed his lips together and started to talk, his words suddenly cut off at the sight of Bob trying to torpedo a large yellow rubber duck.

"Bob."

"What? Ah, got him!"

"Will you at least look as if you're listening to me? It is important."

"All right, just make it quick, the whale gets it next."

"I think you ought to know something."

"About the recent drowning?"

"Murder."

"We don't have the post mortem results yet, so as far as I'm concerned it's a drowning."

"But ..."

"We have a body in a bag with lungs full of water. We have a drunk's story that the Glashton, a mythical creature that lured young virgins to their death with promises of marriage and unlimited wealth and not necessarily in that order, attacked said body and dragged it out to sea. I mean to say – the Glashton!"

"What if Harold did see it?"

"See what? You honestly want me to believe that some ancient marine monster has started haunting the coast for easy prey? For one thing, in case you hadn't noticed, the body was most definitely male and, I have every reason to believe, not a virgin."

"Oh, why?"

"Virgins, even male ones, do not normally carry around packs of condoms in not just one but two varieties."

"I beg your pardon?"

"One was strawberry flavoured, the other ribbed with a novelty end."

"Novelty end?"

"Exactly."

"In my day it was sheep's innards."

"Ah well, that's progress for you."

There was a companionable silence as Bob began to stalk a grey propeller-driven shark and Mannanan mused upon novelty ends and why anyone would even want to make an edible condom. His face reddened considerably when he remembered.

"What if he or she …" Mannanan began.

"Who?"

"The murderer. I really do wish your concentration span was longer Bob Callow, even little Emily can hold an intelligent thought longer than you and she's only five."

"Go on then, I'm listening and you've got sixty seconds. Fifty-nine elephants, fifty-eight elephants, fifty-seven …"

Mannanan scowled at him and then turned and stared at the outlet. Bob, following his gaze, saw to his horror something black and snake-like squirm through the round outlet hole of the bath. It raised its serpent head, yawned showing two sharp hook like teeth and a long red tongue and slipped into the bath. Bob launched himself out of the water and dripping gently, stared in horrified fascination as the snake wrapped itself around the small grey submarine and then disappeared, carrying his favourite bathtime toy below the blue, bubble-covered surface.

"How the bloody hell did you do that?" Bob gasped.

"Just a little trick of the trade," Mannanan replied smugly. "Now, do I have your attention?"

"Yes." Bob reached for a large towel and moving carefully towards the tap end, grabbed the plug chain and pulled. Gradually the level of the water dropped. By degrees, a collection of plastic and rubber shapes appeared at the bottom of the bath. The snake however had drained away with the water.

"My undivided attention."

"Good. Firstly, Harold did see what he honestly believed

to be the Glashton attack and pull to his death a young man, who in my opinion was on borrowed time anyway."

Bob started to speak but was silenced by a single glare. "Secondly," Mannanan continued, "it all has something to do with Sir Arthur Felton. What, I'm not sure as yet."

'Or at least,' Mannanan mused silently, 'nothing that you would as yet believe.'

"Oh?"

"Tavistock is beginning to see things again and they all focus around Sir Arthur. I believe that someone has unfinished business which dates back to possibly the war years, maybe even further back than that. Sir Arthur is the key. I just don't have any idea as to which mystery he will unlock." Mannanan waited to see whether the fish would bite.

"Great!"

"Do I detect a touch of sarcasm? Because if I do ..." The threat was left hanging in the air. Bob looked uneasily towards the now empty bath and shuffled in a crab-like fashion to the door.

"I'll go have a word with Tavistock then and tell Brian to continue searching for amphibious monsters covered in dead fish and seaweed."

"Good. He can start with that film unit," Mannanan replied, sitting back down upon the fluffy blue towelling toilet seat cover.

"What film unit?"

"The one remaking the story of the Glashton. I'm sure they must have at least one Glashton costume complete with seaweed and the odd fish bone."

"Costume!"

"Tavistock was writing the screenplay but she resigned."

"Why does no one tell me anything?" Bob cried despairingly.

"So you believe poor Harold now?"

"Anything else you think I need to know before I march round to the office and start rattling cages?"

"No, I think that's it," Mannanan mused, thoughtfully stroking his chin. Then before fading and with eyes twinkling added, "For now."

Bob stood by the door and shivered. He had to choose between dead sheep, mythical monsters and drowned strangers or repainting the hall and fixing a large water pump to what looked suspiciously like a slate headstone. There was absolutely no doubt in his mind, that if he did go back to work, Moira would probably not speak to him for days. On the other hand the pump's instructions appeared to be in Swahili and he was bound to bugger it up completely. Bob opened the door and tiptoed carefully towards the bedroom whistling "Hi ho, hi ho. It's off to work we go," as he navigated his way around the electric drill, workbench and assorted pots of paint cluttering up the landing.

***

Bob rubbed his hands together and grinned at young Duncan, his newly assigned detective constable. It was odd how they all looked so young now, young and somewhat gormless. Still, Bob always enjoyed a challenge. Whether Duncan would stay the course was a different matter. He was weighing up the probability of Duncan being able to produce a decent cup of tea when Brian entered the office, bowed down with files. Brian stopped and glared at his superior before dumping the assortment of plastic and paper on his desk.

"You don't look a happy lad," Bob said, gaily stating the obvious.

Duncan shuffled uneasily and glanced nervously from

one to the other.

"I thought ..." Brian began cautiously, turning the words over in his brain before uttering, "you were on two weeks' leave. I actually had plans for tonight."

"I know lad, I know and this won't take long. Just wanted to come in and issue a few instructions for tomorrow, so you can both toddle off bright and early to garner a bit of information."

"How early?" Brian asked warily.

"Oh, about half five should do it."

Duncan and Brian exchanged brief looks of horror and Bob's grin became broader.

"Half five!" Brian almost shouted. "Who are we going to interview, Douglas Corporation's nocturnal dustmen?"

"Not exactly, although it may come to going through bins if we can't get any further information about Harold's body and what sick sod has been reading too much Mario Puzo."

"Perhaps he couldn't get hold of a horse, sir?" Duncan observed, his face a picture of youthful innocence.

"You trying to be funny, lad?" Bob asked.

"So why the early start?" Brian hurriedly chipped in.

"Well ... Oh for heaven's sake sit down, the pair of you. You look like a bunch of adolescents waiting for the headmaster to administer a bit of corporal punishment! Normally I wouldn't mind lads, but it just so happens that I left the whip and funny trousers at home."

Brian and Duncan sank into their respective chairs, which left Bob free to pace the room. Bob had become almost immune to the fact that Brian was not in any way small but standing next to both Brian and Duncan was almost too physically challenging. Bob, no midget himself, felt almost dwarfed by Duncan's gangly six foot four inch height. That and the fact that he didn't look old enough to be out of the sixth form.

Bob collected his thoughts and then turned on them with the sort of smile Hannibal Lecter would have given a plate of chopped liver and falafel beans.

"Tomorrow I want you both down at the sea terminal where the latest load of movie-makers are filming scenes for their newest blockbuster based on the story of the Glashton. If our witness is to be believed, someone dressed as the Glashton murdered some poor sod taking a moonlit stroll along one of our less salubrious beaches. Which rather begs the question of why the said victim was actually there? Your mission is to find out what the costume looked like, see if Harold can identify it and get a list of anyone who had access. Oh, and while you're about it, make sure there isn't a spare diving suit which might have looked like our primordial swamp monster. Next, you had better check around and see if anyone knows our body. Oh, and after that you can chase up anything forensic have on the sheep's head, and Brian, you can have a word with the lads and lasses in pathology and find out if they have any idea as to how our cadaver died. They may even have managed to find something which could help us to identify him. Then I want you to liase with the Isle of Man newspapers, Border TV and Manx Radio and see if anyone out there in the big bad world has any information. If we can find out who our body is we'll be nearer to why he died. I don't like someone mooching about on my island thinking he can get away with murder. Right that's it. Off you go and remember …"

Duncan and Brian watched with mounting horror as Bob uttered the immortal words, "Be careful out there!"

Having had his fun, Bob sauntered out, hands thrust deep in his pockets and a spring in his step. Constable baiting was one of the few sports he could still enjoy and it was free.

Brian sighed heavily and stood up.

"Does he do a lot of that?" Duncan asked.

"What?"

"Make sad quotes from the time of the dinosaurs."

"Yes."

"My dad does that, he thinks it's funny too."

"Bob's all right really, apart from the jokes. Just remember two things and you'll be fine. One, never light a cigarette in his presence …"

"Why?"

"Bob's a reformed smoker and he'll frog-march you over to the green cabinet where he keeps a jar full of wet dogends and tar, then he'll give you the lecture and show you the pathology photographs of what your lungs will look like in twenty years time. The last poor sod who lit up in his presence is still receiving counselling."

"That's sick." Duncan swallowed nervously and threw an uncertain glance at the up to the now totally ordinary-looking filing cabinet, which appeared to have been shoe-horned into the far corner of the room. "And the second?" he tentatively asked.

"Never answer back."

"Right," Duncan readily agreed.

"Apart from that, he's not a bad boss, as bosses go. He's fair, always gives credit where credit's due, has a pathological dislike of politicians and never forgets when it's his round. Speaking of which, mine's a bitter top and it's your shout."

Brian, feeling much happier now that he realised that he too could scrounge drinks off this poor unsuspecting sod even further down the food chain than he was, shrugged himself back into his jacket and sauntered from the office.

***

Half an hour later Bob was lavishly anointing fish and

chips with malt vinegar and trying to persuade Tavistock to have a look at the collection of papers he'd been given by Constance.

Richard Allan, seeing them edging towards some sort of agreement, finished his chips and gathering his brood around him, bustled them upstairs to be bathed, brushed and deposited in their respective beds.

"So, I thought you could just have a look at it and see if you think it's got anything to do with our body," Bob muttered indistinctly whilst chewing a piece of fish.

"Why?" Tavistock asked, trying not to look at a particularly sticky bit of batter stuck to Bob's upper lip.

"I dunno, I just have this feeling that it might."

"But Sir Arthur said it was a load of ..."

"Well he would, wouldn't he?"

"Give it here then."

Bob handed over the brown envelope and the sheets of paper covered in a fine clear plastic and watched carefully as Tavistock gingerly separated the pages and began to read.

"Well?" he asked impatiently, studying her face.

"Well what?"

"So, what do you feel?"

"Nothing."

"Nothing!"

"That's right, not a proverbial sausage, not even a psychic twitch!"

"Oh."

"What did you expect me to do? Go into a coma and start spouting drivel with strands of ectoplasm emanating from my suddenly possessed body?" Tavistock exclaimed, pushing the papers back to him, across the table. "Honestly Bob! What do you think I am, a music hall turn or some sort of private freak show?"

"I was hoping you'd see something," Bob declared, his

voice sulky with disappointment.

"Well I didn't," Tavistock rose and moved to the fridge.

"Want a lager?" she asked.

"Only one, I'm driving."

Tavistock removed two, small, squat bottles of French beer and pushed the door of the fridge shut with her foot. Handing one to Bob with a glass she leant over and pinched a chip.

"Oi, you've had yours," Bob growled, reaching for the bottle opener, which sat in the middle of the pine table surrounded by little metal lids.

"Mind you, that's odd in itself ..." Tavistock mused.

"Why?" Bob asked, a fine moustache of white foam hanging from his upper lip, the batter having now been located by tongue and swallowed.

"Not feeling anything. Today, at Sir Arthur's I was only glancing through an old letter and I got some images clear and bright."

"Perhaps it's the plastic, stops the vibrations or whatever."

"Wouldn't have thought it would have made much difference. It hasn't before. Normally I'd pick up something, however vague."

"So what do you think then?"

"Well for what its worth, I don't think that the information here is actually based on fact. Part of it is very likely true but it's missing a fundamental piece of information."

"Such as?"

"The riots happened. The Finn was definitely stabbed. But not by Sir Arthur. There are gaps here. For instance how do they know who was killed in the riot? What if the victim was somebody else? Put it this way, the original letter was written by a blackmailer who wasn't even born when all this happened, which he freely admits on the top of the copied notes. The newspaper cuttings are recent copies included in a millennium souvenir supplement. And the copied notes are just that. Even the so-called letter from Charles Cholmondley, to some guy in Cairo, is an old carbon copy. What we really need are the originals or something that actually belonged to someone actively involved with these specific events."

"Makes sense. So if I can dig up the originals then you could do the coma and time travel bit." Bob sat up, feeling much brighter and almost back to his normally devious self.

"Maybe," Tavistock reluctantly agreed.

"Good." Bob rose and gulping down the last of the beer, muttered his thanks and departed, looking thoughtful. Richard returned to the kitchen in time to wave goodbye and watch as Bob ambled across the twilit drive towards his car.

"So he's finally remembered he does have a home to go to?" Richard asked in all innocence. "And by now the light is definitely too bad to paint in," he added, a wicked gleam in his eye. Tavistock giggled and quietly closed the back door, shutting out the deepening night and the sounds of rooks settling down in the tall trees bordering the lawn.

***

Brian lay entwined around the small slim body of his fiancée and heaved a very self-satisfied sigh.

"That was really good," he stated, kissing the top of her head and breathing in the faint aroma of shampoo and the perfume she habitually wore.

"Really?" Caroline asked a trifle smugly, as she settled herself further into the shape of his body.

"Really," he agreed.

"Now I wonder if Sir means the casserole or the sex?" she asked, a wicked glint in her eyes.

"The casserole of course, mind you the sex wasn't bad." Brian chuckled, now nuzzling her ears.

"Stop it you," Caroline admonished. "Or I'll have to teach you how to behave!"

"Promises, promises," Brian muttered drowsily. "Are you going to dress up as Nursy and do I get to beat you with soggy vegetables?"

"Brian!"

"Yes dear?"

"I have a horrible feeling you are going to grow up just like Uncle Bob."

"That's what I was going to tell you," Brian said sitting bolt upright.

"What?" Caroline mumbled sleepily.

"Bob has agreed to give you away."

Caroline wriggled further under the duvet and sighed contentedly. "Great. Now I don't have to ring the old man and ask him to do it, not that he would," she muttered.

"You have told him? Haven't you?" Brian asked suspiciously.

"Er ..."

"Oh, Caroline. Have you told anyone?"

"Yes," Caroline replied, stung. "I've told everyone; my mum, my friends and all my elderly relatives. I just didn't see the point in telling some sad bastard who walked out on me when I was two. Someone who occasionally manages to remember Christmas! But never, I hasten to add, my birthday."

"Ah."

"Anyway I'd much prefer Bob to give me away." Caroline paused and then thoughtfully asked. "So if Bob is giving me away, who is going to be your best man?"

"Bob."

"Bob! Can he do both?"

"He seems to think he can." Brian stretched the full length of the bed and yawned. "He said we'd have to discuss it with the vicar."

"The vicar!" Caroline shot her head out from under the duvet just as Brian was fumbling for the switch on the bedside table.

"Oh, no you don't, Buster! I thought we had agreed to a quiet registry office."

"Ah ..." Brian pulled a pillow over his head and pretended to snore.

"Are you trying to say that after our lengthy discussion between the lamb casserole and the cherry pie that you have decided we are going to get married in church!"

"Sort of. I was trying to get around to discussing it."

Brian lifted the pillow from his face just enough to be glared at balefully by his beloved.

"You are a prime pig!" Caroline snorted.

"Does this mean yes?" Brian asked hopefully. There was a long pause in which Caroline rolled a conversation she had had with her mother that afternoon, around her head.

"All right, all right, I have to admit that Mum would be happier. She didn't much care for the civil ceremony thing. Seemed to think only divorcees and heretics ever got married that way."

"You don't mind?"

"No, not really. I suppose it means we will have to go the whole hog," Caroline mused, sitting up and wrapping her arms around her knees. She looked, Brian thought to himself, like an elfin extra from a 'Midsummer's Night's Dream'.

"The whole hog, what exactly do you mean?"

"Well." Caroline looked him straight in the eye, a picture of studied innocence. "Long white dress with matching veil for me. Top hat and tails for you. Flowers, bells, reception, five or six bridesmaids, big car ..."

"Hang on a minute, just exactly how much is all that going to cost?"

"According to Fiona, who got married last year, about twenty grand."

"What!" Brian exploded, spluttering.

"But I'm sure we can cut a lot of corners and I'll only have one or maybe two bridesmaids." Caroline grinned at him and then lent down and kissed him firmly on the lips.

Brian tried to come up for air and failed miserably, one particular body part turning traitor almost as soon as Caroline had leant over him, exposing a certain amount of rounded perfumed flesh and rose-red nipples.

"That's my big boy," Caroline murmured appreciatively. "Just you come to mama."

Brian gave up, all thoughts being temporarily suspended until further notice.

Later, as they slept, he dreamt that he was being pulled out to sea by a sea serpent wearing a veil. Bob Callow was standing on a rock calling to him from out of a large shell-pink megaphone. He couldn't make out what he was saying but a part of him knew it had something to do with the vicar and a large bill for tea and sandwiches.

Chapter 7

Duncan groaned as the alarm clock bounced on the bedside table beside him. He tried putting a pillow over his head but the insistent bleeping of the little plastic model of Thunderbird Two could still be heard. Any moment now the lights would flash and a disembodied voice would declare that Thunderbirds were go. Duncan blearily switched on the overhead light and now firmly on autopilot, tried to disconnect his parents' warped idea of a leaving-home present. "What did I ever do to them?" he muttered, grabbing a striped towelling dressing gown from the floor.

Duncan peered myopically around the small bedroom and after locating his glasses, on his landlord's apology for a dressing table, padded into the shower room.

After the minimum contact with water necessary to clear any body odours, Duncan dressed hurriedly and emerged from his flat five minutes later, still dripping and looking anything but bright-eyed and bushy-tailed. Brian was already waiting for him in his car, as were the first of the day's seagulls who were perched in single file along the guttering of his attic flat. Duncan looked up as they screamed profanities at him and one just managed to get the corner of his freshly dry cleaned jacket with a gob of white and black goo.

Duncan swore and Brian, feeling older by the day passed him a white, slightly soggy cloth as he closed the car door.

"Bloody birds!" Duncan swore, wiping furiously at the stain which to his surprise was actually coming off.

"Have another."

"Thanks. This stuff really works."

"Baby wipes, my sister swears by them. Frankly, if they can clean up the nuclear waste that erupts from the average newborn's bum, they can clear up most things." Brian started the car and moved away from the kerb. "Before you came out, round here was like a scene from Hitchcock's 'The Birds'. Have you been upsetting the local wildlife or something?" Brian asked, squealing to a halt as a black tailless cat sauntered across the road in front of him.

"Shite hawks we call 'em back home."

"I presume you don't like seagulls then?"

Duncan shook his head but still managed to appear vaguely guilty. Bob, observing the look, asked in the manner of one interviewing the prime suspect, "You'd better come clean lad, before someone from the animal rights groups gets a whiff. After all, we can always offer you a bit of police protection." Brian let the words hang and Duncan shuffled uneasily.

"I fed them a few sandwiches and they seem to have taken a dislike to me."

"What sort of sandwiches?" Brian asked, intrigued.

"English mustard and tabasco."

Brian gave vent to a short snort of mirth. "What sort of bread?" he asked, curious as to just exactly how far his new junior would go to alienate the local wildlife.

"Organic brown stuff. It were a bit mouldy but well, I was annoyed, I'd just put the washing out and they ..."

"Well next time be a bit more careful. Manx gulls have a long memory and they talk to each other."

"How do you make that out?"

"Well yesterday there was only two or three sitting on your roof. Today it was the full cast of Jonathan Livingstone Seagull ... You work it out."

Duncan sat beside him and chewed his bottom lip in a thoughtful fashion. "What if I do them a proper feed of chips? I could do them a butty with white bread."

Brian considered this option with mock seriousness before replying. "That might work. On the other hand you could always move to somewhere without gulls, like the Gobi Desert."

"I knew I'd love working here. The people are dead friendly."

Brian chuckled; he had a horrible feeling that Caroline was right and he really was turning into Bob Callow. There was a peaceful silence as they drove on past the law courts, down the hill and onto the promenade. Turning to the right they narrowly missed a bright orange bus, which hooted loudly at him. Brian hastily applied the brakes and exulting loudly reversed into a parking space, right outside the Sea Terminal building.

"Here we are then. Welcome to my favourite building, the truly spectacular and one of a kind, lemon squeezer." Brian announced.

"What?" Duncan asked, puzzled.

Brian pointed at the building in front of them and began writing a note to the resident traffic warden.

"While I'm locking up, finishing this and collecting the files, you walk across the road, stand on the pavement the other side, look back at me and you will see that this fine edifice has all the charm and spontaneity of the average juice extractor. Which is probably why the Department of Tourism has dibs on the offices here."

Duncan watched him for signs of a wind-up and seeing none, trotted off. He returned a few minutes later grinning from ear to ear.

"You're right, it does look like a lemon squeezer and I thought you lot had no sense of humour!"

"This from a man that wears a skirt complete with stuffed guinea pig. A man, who not only eats the haggis, but plays tunes on its mortal remains and actually believes that the pillocks at Westminster will leave them alone. Even though we believe in fairies and have cats with no tails, even though we have miles of water between us and them, we never fell for that one!"

"Point taken."

"Good, now I make it five thirty on the nail and somewhere around here is a PA called Anne Swales who will, I hope, explain all there is to know about the making of the average teen nightmare. And here she is." Brian stood to attention and carefully locked the car door. As a woman of uncertain years marched purposely towards them.

The lady in question was not the glamour puss Duncan had envisaged but a short, rather stocky female, who looked suspiciously like his old history teacher. She even had the same taste in plain but serviceable clothing right down to the mottled green ribbed tights and the woollen liberty print scarf wrapped around her head.

"Good!" the woman announced in the sort of voice that would have had no problems in being heard across at least two playing fields. "You're on time although I don't expect anyone else is. You got your thermals on?" she asked, squinting up at them.

"Thermals?" Duncan asked bemusedly.

"Yes young man. It gets a bit parky doing nothing except standing around waiting for the next crisis to hit. Mind you, you sound like a nice wee Scottie so you're probably used to it eh?" Duncan exchanged horrified looks with Brian, who unearthed an old notebook, which he pointedly opened.

"I thought these films were like one big party?" Duncan whispered to Brian as Anne turned smartly on her heel and proceeded to march around the side of the Sea Terminal building, towards a large white and black trailer with enough aerials on the roof to keep a NASA anorak happy. Without so much as a backward glance to check that they were keeping up she disappeared inside, closely followed by Brian and Duncan.

Within the crowded metallic walls they found a plethora of technical equipment, monitors, soundboards and a small table complete with tea and coffee-making facilities consisting of one plastic kettle, a collection of sachets and a motley assortment of brown stained mugs.

"Want a cuppa?" Anne asked, plugging the kettle in.

"Er, yes please, didn't have time for breakfast," Duncan muttered as Brian raised an enquiring eyebrow.

"So which part of Scotland are you from?" Anne asked conversationally as she wiped the insides of two mugs with a greying towel. "Only you don't sound like you come from Glasgow, which is where most of our sound crew are from," she added in explanation as Duncan was watching her with a fixed blank expression.

"Er, well I'm from Perth but went to St Andrews and they tend to beat an accent out of you. I guess you could call it an Edinburgh burr," he added helpfully.

"Right, well there you go, one cup of hot water, just add any of the packets to it and you may end up with something vaguely drinkable," Anne smiled as she handed over the semi-clean Bart Simpson mug and turned back to Brian. Duncan dubiously examined the inside and with a quick shrug decided he did really need at least a small strong shot of caffeine. He just prayed that it wasn't going to be laced with some non-specific form of food poisoning.

"Now then, what is it you want to know?" Anne asked, seating herself down upon a grey and somewhat stained swivel chair.

"We wondered if you could tell us if it would be possible for anyone to sneak out with one of your costumes?" Brian enquired, settling into a large brown sagging armchair.

"Well, I suppose someone on the set could," she replied after careful consideration and then curiosity getting the better of her asked, "and which costume were you thinking of?"

"The Glashton," Brian replied.

"Well, now there you have me. Frankly I'd say no, off the top of my head but Wardrobe would maybe make a better assessment."

"Why so sure?"

"Well ..." Anne thoughtfully sipped her drink. "The thing is that particular costume is actually fairly heavy; it has to be, as it's weighted and has to look good for the underwater shots. But one of the main reasons would be because it's been handmade for the actor concerned so I guess it would only fit him. Another consideration is that it's the only costume with very tight security. It was pretty costly as costumes go and we couldn't easily afford another, not on what's now left of our budget. Our wardrobe mistress would be a better person to ask."

"So where could we find her?"

"Him. He's called Rob. Sorry, I always call them mistresses, habit I guess. He should be in the wardrobe van setting up for the extras. This morning's filming calls for an old-fashioned costume set, so it may be fairly hectic. But the Glashton doesn't make an appearance so he can show you the actual costume and our security system. We have a CCTV camera installed in there to ensure that nothing gets, er, borrowed. I'll be happy to introduce him to you if you like."

They left the safe warmth of the lorry to be greeted by a bitingly cold wind, which blew off the sea and had echoes of Siberia in it. Duncan shivered and pulled his coat tighter. He was, after all, used to the cold but the winds of the Island were not only cold but also very damp. The sort of wind that ought to have been wrung out properly before being allowed out. Anne marched off towards a sprawl of vans and trailers parked at the side of the quay. People milled around, some in period costume of a date somewhere between the Restoration and the Victorian era, whilst others were moving huge silver screens and arc lamps. A young man with a collection of body rings and dreadlocks, carrying what looked like several miles of thick black plastic cable shouted to them to mind the boom. Anne, looking upwards, ducked, swore and pointing them in the direction of a long silver trailer left them, to have words, as she put it, with someone called the gaffer.

Brian shrugged and knocking firmly on the door of the trailer, entered without waiting for a reply. Duncan following swiftly behind, nearly lost his balance as he navigated the step to be greeted by a young lady of noble proportions who was having her ample breasts pushed into a corset which looked at least two sizes too small. Duncan swallowed, reddened and coughed. He did try to look away but discovered to his horror that the van was full of mirrors and about eight other ladies of various sizes were doing exactly the same with their costumes, which even Penthouse would have called skimpy.

"Er, sorry to bother you ladies but we were looking for someone called Rob," Brian stated totally unfazed.

"Well, you've found him," muttered a voice appearing from under the skirts of a large lady, who was patiently bending over a chair.

"Well love, that's the best I can do for now." Waving

a pair of wire clippers at them, Rob began to pull and tie the ribbons around the top of the woman's skirt. "These wretched things. You can never get the bustle in the right place and if you do manage it the bones in the side panels slip. I don't know who made this little lot but they should be shot.,,

"Right," Brian replied, nonplussed.

"Ten minutes, ladies!" shouted a voice from outside. There was a sudden flurry of skirts and a whisper of silk as wraps and large baggy cardigans were grabbed. Brian and Duncan huddled against the wall as bodies pushed them aside in a mass exodus towards the door. With a metallic bang the door closed and peace settled around them.

"So," Rob said, beginning to clear up the debris of pins and oddments of materials scattering the floor and narrow counters lining the walls. "Two questions, the first being who the hell are you and how did you get past security and two, what do you want?"

Brian flashed his warrant card at him and grinned at Rob's stunned expression. "The answer to question one is that we are police officers investigating a recent drowning and two, we were wondering if we could have a look at your costume for the Glashton."

"Oh. Right, well, enough said. It's in there, help yourself." Rob pointed to a tall metal cabinet and after searching various pockets presented them with a small silver key.

Brian unlocked the door and the smell, which hit him as the door swung open, immediately had all three backed against the wall.

"What in heaven's name is that?" Rob asked, gagging.

"Some sort of fish. I hope." Duncan muttered, his eyes watering.

Brian, covering his mouth and nose with a large cotton handkerchief inspected the costume visually before closing the door and re-locking the cabinet. Rob and Duncan breathed a sigh of relief as Brian punched numbers on his mobile.

"I gather from your expression of surprise that that particular costume doesn't always smell that bad?" Duncan stated.

"Not at all, I only cleaned it down the day before yesterday, you have to wash it down with a little water because of the sand, the poor chap that has to wear it gets this terrible bright red rash if I don't. It's made out of rubber and a type of honeycombed latex foam with lead weights. I suppose it must be like trying to act from inside a large thick plastic bag. It does get really quite unpleasantly hot inside and so the actor is usually naked bar this thong thing he wears. Well, as you can no doubt imagine a few grains of salty sand would tend to irritate after a bit. Especially as it takes about an hour or so to fit it on and then apply the head and hand makeup."

"So it wouldn't be all that easy for someone else to put it on and wear it?"

"Not unless he or she were the same size and they would almost certainly need a bit of help to get into it." Rob considered his answer for a minute or two and then added as an afterthought, "It does actually zip up at the front so I suppose someone could have got it on by themselves, but they'd have a lot of difficulty with the head."

"Oh?" Duncan prompted.

"You see it slips over the neck, just like an old-fashioned diving mask and is attached to an air hose at the back. You really need two people to fit it properly, as the neck and the head have to be almost screwed together. The other thing is we don't normally fit it on in here but on the beach or the outside of the tank, because of the weight. It's really designed to move in the water, nobody could possibly move around in it on land, or at least not for any distance."

"But you think someone could have taken it, judging from the smell?" Brian urged, having finished his hurried conversation.

"Well yes, wouldn't you? I mean – I clean it, put it back fresh as a daisy and then find it stinking worse than a trawler after a week at sea in a heatwave." Rob sighed. "And before you ask, the production team PA and I have the only keys. And those keys stay upon our persons at all times. Apart from when we bathe, in which case I leave mine on a hook on the bathroom door."

"Well that appears to be that, for the moment at least." Brian muttered, switching off his mobile and making a few hastily scribbled notes before returning both to the snug confines of his jacket. "I've just spoken to Geoff from forensic and he and his lads will be down shortly. Please don't touch anything, Duncan will stay here and make sure nothing gets moved. Not that it would," he added hastily, seeing the outraged expression on Rob's face. "I'll go and have a word with Anne and if you could give me a list of everyone who has been in and out of here since you put the cleaned costume back it would be a big help. Duncan, I'll see you later."

Smiling broadly at the look of consternation on Duncan's face, Brian departed smartly for the wealth of fresh air outside.

It was some ten minutes later that Brian stood leaning against the grey concrete harbour wall and watched a cormorant diving amongst the waves just outside the harbour entrance. Just as he was about to worry that it would never reappear again, it would rise phoenix-like and look around, head held to one side, beak at the ready for the next fish. Out past the ridge of sharp black rocks sat the Tower of Refuge, a scaled-down, Victorian version of a Scottish tower house complete with turret. It squatted protectively upon a roughly hewn sprawl of dark granite, a red flag with a bright yellow design of three dancing legs flapping jauntily from a short, gold-tipped flagpole. Someone coughed beside him, bouncing his brain from its reverie and the ever-growing invitation list he was beginning to formulate, in an as yet little-used corner of his brain.

"What?" Brian squawked, spinning round.

"Penny for them?" asked the man. Brian looked him up and down and backed towards the wall. Long leather coats he could just about accept as male attire. Floppy silk shirts with sleeves the average orang-utan would find inconveniently long he could almost be reasonable with. It was the bright emerald green velvet hat and the orange feather he was finding a certain amount of difficulty relaxing with. That and the fact that the shirt was pink, a sort of Barbie pink, the colour all little girls loved from the age of three or four, until the time they grew up which seemed to Brian to be nearer nine than nineteen these days. All in all the man looked like a particularly tall, brightly coloured, wrinkled leprechaun, and an extremely camp one at that.

"Er ..." Brian spluttered.

"You're not one of the crew, are you?" the man asked, moving a step nearer.

Brian, wary as a turkey two weeks before Christmas, growled, "No," and took a hasty step backwards.

"Ah, didn't think so," said the man, delving into the folds of leather. Fascinated, Brian watched as a pipe, tobacco pouch and lighter were extracted.

"My name's Sam, Samuel Lawrence. I am that poorly paid and little thanked creature known as the film historian and adviser to this particular world of film and television. My job is to produce a cornucopia of little known facts and at times and depending on the director of the moment, a selection of downright lies. And you are?" Samuel paused, waiting for Brian to reply.

"Brian Clague, I'm a policeman."

"Ah, CID?" Samuel breathed with a certain amount of relish, whilst pushing strands of tobacco down into the bowl of the pipe.

"Yes."

"Not a man of conversation are you my dear?" Samuel grinned and with total concentration applied the lighter flame at a carefully held angle. The tobacco caught and Samuel put the stem to his lips and puffed. The acrid smell of mellow Virginian tobacco filled the surrounding air and Samuel Lawrence lounged gracefully against the sea wall, his back to the prevailing wind.

Brian watched him and on sudden impulse asked.

"I don't suppose you have much to do with wardrobe?"

"Me?" Samuel removed the stem of his pipe and looked at the bowl in a sorrowful fashion. Brian, observing the craggy features of the face, saw something, some emotion, briefly cross Samuel's face. Samuel smiled, his lips turning upwards and the small pencil-thin moustache quivered. The smile, however, did not reach the eyes, a small piece of information that was duly noted by Brian and stored in his little grey cells for future reference.

"Of course I do Officer. I have to give my opinion on all sorts of historical questions; for instance whether you can get away with wearing a digital watch with a seventeenth-century lace cuff. Or heeled shoes with a ruby buckle. Of course they could have been stolen, but really you'd think Rob would have had more sense."

"Sorry?" Brian asked, his face a study in incomprehension.

Samuel, slyly watching Brian's confusion, emitted a high-pitched titter of mirth.

"You don't know, do you? Ah well, why should you? I

give advice on what sort of characters would wear what sort of costume. I have to take into account social standing, the amount of money they may have had. How fashionable they were. What type of cloth and other materials were available etc, etc. Believe it or not it's quite an art. You wouldn't believe how many people watch the finished product just so that they can point out the things that are wrong." He sighed and tapped the bowl of his pipe against the grey concrete wall.

"Do you advise on other things?" Brian asked.

"Oh yes. For instance, I dig up information about the times we are dealing with, type of houses, how they would eat, etc. My speciality is in finding any old legends or historical characters we could bring in."

"Must be interesting," Brian prompted, keeping his voice carefully neutral.

"Very much so. To be honest, your Island is so rich in tales of magic, monsters and frankly murder that I'm seriously thinking of staying on and writing a book. All that new age, Celtic stuff is very popular with the reading public you know. Yes, I think I could knock up a fairly lucrative tome, if I stay." Samuel frowned, the eyes momentarily hooded by blue-veined lids.

"Don't suppose you'd be interested in something a bit more modern," Brian asked.

"How do you mean?" Samuel replied, looking directly into Brian's eyes. Brian held his gaze and then looked away towards the cormorant.

"We had a lot going on over here during the First and Second World Wars. Lots of tales of derring-do, murder, riots and escapes."

"Really? How interesting. However I must admit I'd prefer something a little older a little more cerebral. Besides, such a lot has been written already that I'm not sure I'd come up with anything of major commercial interest. But I will, of course, keep your suggestion in mind."

"How about the story of the Tidemaster?" Brian asked, all innocence.

"The who?" For a fraction of a second Samuel hesitated, his body suddenly taut.

"The Tidemaster. Now why did I say that? Must have picked the expression up somewhere." Brian stuffed his hands in his pockets and shivered. "Well better be off, have to find Anne before that lot from forensic turn up. Good to meet you, sir."

Samuel watched him turn and walk away. His eyes were their usual unfathomable granite grey but his mind was whirling with possibilities.

***

Nigel Moore, the youngest member of the forensic team, leant against the side of the metal trailer and breathed in the crisp, freshly squeezed air with a look of absolute and total rapture. He was in the process of taking the first long drags from a cigarette when Duncan slowly approached him, sipping cautiously from the newly refilled Bart Simpson mug.

Nigel, surveying Duncan's height from his own five foot five inches, carefully tried to hide the smoking white stick behind his back. Duncan, watching him, decided that Nigel looked like a small, sallow, emaciated ferret, but a ferret he might possibly be able to glean a bit of useful information from.

"It's all right, Bob's on holiday," Duncan brightly informed him, taking another small sip of scalding coffee.

Nigel visibly relaxed and carefully took another long pull on his cigarette.

"He wasn't yesterday, at the airport," Nigel muttered with a frown.

"No, but he is now – or at least," Duncan informed him. "He's not either here or in the office."

"Doesn't mean to say he won't be," Nigel replied, looking furtively around. "Geoff, that's my boss, reckons Bob Callow has a sixth sense when there's trouble about. He always says that if you had twelve dustbins all in a row, Bob Callow would be able to go straight to the one with the evidence in, just as if he had X-ray vision."

"Oh."

"Do you want a fag?" Nigel asked.

"No thanks, don't smoke," Duncan replied. "Just as well, really," he added in a thoughtful fashion remembering the cabinet.

"Why do you think they done it?" Nigel asked, pointing to the trailer behind them.

"Done what?" Duncan asked.

"Stuck that wretched crab in the costume."

"Dunno."

"I think they put it there to hide the other stuff." Nigel lowered his voice to almost a whisper. "I bet you anything you like that, someone was wearing that costume as a disguise. Just so that they couldn't be recognised, when they drowned that chap the other night."

"You don't say," Duncan replied, his eyes wide and wary.

"Of course we'll have 'em." Nigel took in one last long gulp of nicotine-flavoured smoke and dropped the butt on the ground. "There's not much gets past us," he added, grinding the remains of the cigarette into the tarmac with the heel of his shoe.

"What sort of stuff?" Duncan asked curiously.

"Well, I'm not sure I should say anything really, the report hasn't been done yet and Geoff …"

His voice tailed off as he checked that there was no one else around to overhear. "There was a bit of scraped skin in the creases of the wristbands and traces of other stuff on the neck. So it looks like whoever it was they were trying to drown, put up a bit of a fight. And the really interesting bit is ..."

"Yes," Duncan eagerly prompted.

"There were these odd reddish hairs caught up in the zip and Geoff reckons he's seen them before."

"Where?" Duncan squeaked.

"In the suitcase," Nigel informed him with a sly smile. "The one we found the sheep's head in!"

"What!" Duncan exclaimed.

"Yeah, curious bit of information that. Wonder what super sleuth will make of it, eh?" Nigel grinned at him. A van approaching from the car park flashed its lights and then slowed to a halt in front of them. Nigel sighed heavily and picked up the discarded backpack before climbing into the impatiently waiting vehicle.

Duncan watched him drive off and finished the last of his coffee.

If Nigel was actually right about the hairs, it would mean that both the drowning and the decapitated head could be connected – but why? Duncan shook his head and trotted back towards Anne's trailer, his head positively bursting with theories.

***

Bob thoughtfully replaced the receiver and then gleefully rubbed his hands. Brian, sitting at his usual desk squashed against the wall, turned the next sheet of paper over and waited.

"Well, you will be pleased to know that the long hand of the law has been set in motion, the dogs of war are unleashed and nemesis approaches," Bob announced.

"Have you been reading again?" Brian enquired

warily.

"No, just talking to the press. Well the news editor but she promises to hold the front page and advise the great unwashed that there is a murderer in our midst who likes drowning people, while wearing seaweed, latex and a monster mask."

"Great, we'll have every weirdo on the Island sticking his hands up and admitting to the crime, as long as they get their fifteen minutes of fame, fortune and press coverage!" Brian grumbled.

"You sound unimpressed. Ah well. I also, in my wisdom, sent them an artist's drawing of the face before death and have asked them to ensure it gets as much coverage as possible. Our unknown should have been staying somewhere, or living with some form of communication with the rest of the world, even if it's only nipping to the shops for a paper and a pint of milk."

"All points bulletin for landladies, eh?" Brian asked, grinning.

"You can laugh lad but there's nothing much gets past the average Manx landlady. If the Spanish Inquisition had had one of those stalwarts of interrogation, they wouldn't have needed to invent the rack. Just let 'em loose with a pot of tea and plate of buttered scones and you'd tell 'em anything just to get out!"

"True," Brian agreed, going back to his papers.

They sat in companionable silence, Brian reading and Bob staring out of the window. A noise not unlike that of an approaching legion of Roman soldiers was heard striding along the corridor.

"Duncan appears to be back," Brian observed.

"I heard. Do you think he does tea?" Bob asked.

"You can but ask," Brian replied, listening for the turn of the doorhandle.

Duncan entered the room and drawing himself to his

full height said, "You wanted to see me sir?"

"Um, yes Duncan. Look, just sit will you?" Bob watched as Duncan folded his long bones into the spare chair, which habitually skulked in a corner. Normally it just sat there due to its propensity to squeak. However it appeared to be totally soundless now. 'Fear probably,' Bob thought to himself. "So, Duncan, how did you enjoy your day in films?"

"It was all right until we found the Glashton costume," Duncan muttered, remembering the smell which, as forensic had discovered, came from the very large, very dead crab caught up in the latex folds. They had not been impressed and there had been a certain amount of grinding and gnashing of teeth as they dusted for prints and hunted for fibres. Although how they could tell the difference between what should or should not have been there, defied him. He wondered briefly about passing on the information about the hairs but decided to do it later when he'd been told what it was that Bob had called him in for.

"Ah, yes," Bob mused.

"Well?" Duncan asked, trying to find a comfortable position and failing.

"Can you make tea?" Bob asked, all innocence. Brian choked back a laugh. Duncan, observing the muffled smiles, glared.

"Yes sir."

"Good, mine's fairly strong ..."

"Think of creosote and you'll be there," Brian muttered. Bob gave him a filthy look, which would have curdled milk, and continued.

"Milk, two sugars and a spoon, because none of you lot ⬦ know how to stir. Brian will have milk and one sugar, and you'd better make one for yourself."

"Anything else?" Duncan asked.

"Nope, that's it unless Brian ... No. That's it then lad,

off you go."

Duncan raised himself from the chair, which finally emitted a faint rusted scream. A bolt fell to the floor followed by a very small spring.

Duncan looked at the debris and then at Bob.

"I couldn't help it," he stuttered.

"I know lad, frankly I'm surprised it's lasted this long. Still now it's officially deceased we could put in for a new one and a desk that matches. So that's three teas and a requisition form."

"Oh."

"You are, you will no doubt be pleased to know, the newest official member of my team and after my most recent chat with the pathologist, on one of the weirdest murder investigations I have ever been assigned to." Brian looked up from his papers.

"Apparently the body on the beach had been partially strangled and then drowned by a person or persons unknown. Geoff also thinks that the suitcase we found the sheep's head in could possibly have belonged to the aforementioned cadaver. Which may possibly tie in with someone who was trying to earn a spot of extra cash by a bit of illicit blackmail. All in all the whole thing is beginning to look like one very large ants' nest and I have no doubt that the boss is going to be positively overjoyed when he gets to hear all the gory details." Bob sat back and scratched the side of his head. Then after fumbling in one of his desk drawers, he stalked over to the wall chart and carefully drew a long thick black line through the remaining week of his holiday.

"Which means," he stated, settling back down at his desk, "that I am from this moment on officially back in charge. Moira is going to be absolutely delighted!"

He huffed loudly and began to chew thoughtfully on the end of the black marker pen.

"Still, she could always get a little man in. Brian," he asked, his voice suddenly brighter, "have you got the phone book? I need the Yellow Pages."

✳ ✳ ✳

Bob and Brian sat in the small boardroom at the Isle of Man Newspaper offices in Peel Road and waited. Back at Police Headquarters Duncan was still wading through copious quantities of witness statements and sitting by the phone, in the forlorn hope that someone, somewhere, would recognise their as yet unknown and unclaimed body. Brian shuffled and took a surreptitious look at his watch. He wasn't, on balance, all that convinced that he had the better deal.

The door opened and the duty editor, known fondly in non-editorial circles as She Who Must Be Obeyed and as something far less flattering by her subordinates, entered the room. She was, thought Brian, an extremely attractive, platinum blonde, thirty something. Not a hair was out of place, her immaculate Chanel-style suit was worn with the sort of power that, a few hundred years earlier, ran large estates and hanged the average itinerant worker without so much as a backward glance.

Gloria Chalmers smiled at Bob with glacial blue eyes and sat down. Brian gulped and visibly reddened, as her navy blue skirt rode up over long, slim, Julia Roberts legs.

Aware of exactly how she could affect the majority of red-blooded males, Gloria crossed her legs, exposing several inches of well-toned thigh.

"So, Bob, what can the press do for you?" The voice, low and husky, asked. Brian bent to his notebook and Bob, well aware of his subordinate's unease, chuckled.

"You could ably assist us by running the picture of the deceased for the next couple of issues and asking if anyone served him a meal, hired him a car or rented him a room. Any chance any of the major papers across could run something? After all, man drowned by sea monster must be some sort of draw, if only for the tabloids?"

"Well ..." Gloria muttered. "I could have a word with a few of my former colleagues. I suppose any sort of byline would help. I checked the film angle by the way and one of the neanderthals is working on a link between the filming of the Glashton and a possible copycat killing. I was wondering though, if you could give us a few words about the decapitated sheep found at the airport. After all the body on the beach is hardly news now it's made the front page and Manx Radio." The words Manx Radio were hissed with such venom that Brian looked up from his notes and then hastily back down, as he met the full force of Gloria's Siamese cat stare.

"Dunno about the sheep, love. Thing is, at the moment it doesn't really have much to do with anything," Bob calmly advised her, despite the fact that he was lying through his teeth.

"Oh I don't know. It is, after all, a highly theatrical way of gaining attention. And from no less a person than our very own son of the people, Ian Felton-Cholmondley."

"I couldn't possibly comment," Bob muttered, more than slightly miffed. "Anyway, how the bloody hell did you find out?" he asked crossly.

"I have my sources."

Bob watched appreciatively as she uncrossed her legs and leant towards him, the white silk blouse she was wearing gaping just enough to enable the unwary viewer to catch a glimpse of serious cleavage. Brian, looking up from his notes, eyeballed the golden glimpse of flesh, reddened further, shifted uncomfortably and bent back to his writing.

"I bet you have," Bob replied. "Unfortunately the

message wasn't aimed at our noble, mentally challenged Euro MP but at his maternal grandfather."

"I know, but since when did the truth get in the way of a good story? Besides, if there is anything dark and malodorous lurking in the Felton cupboards, I'd put money on Ian's involvement."

"You would?" Bob asked, suddenly intensely interested.

"Oh yes," Gloria cooed. "To be perfectly honest, if I thought for a moment that running a story about the sheep and our waterlogged cadaver would seriously embarrass that useless piece of well-shod excrement …"

"Might be a bit too close for your legal department," Bob queried, watching her face. The eyes momentarily sparkled with pure venom as Gloria seriously considered the possibilities. Bob wondered if she was about to have a Medusa moment because from the snarl on her lips and the poisonous look in her eyes all she really lacked were a few snakes writhing around in the golden curls, which were carefully brushed and framing an immaculately painted face.

"Oh, I think I could do something with it. After all, we can always print a retraction in the next issue." Gloria smiled. It was the smile of an extremely well-fed barracuda.

"Besides, who reads obscure paragraphs at the bottom of page 14 a week later?" Bob innocently remarked.

"Exactly."

"Well don't quote us as your sources and don't expect official back-up but a bit of well placed sensationalism might lure something out from under a rock. Perhaps you could make a few discreet enquiries of your own?" Bob asked. Brian looked up from his notes. He hadn't got a clue what they were now talking about and it worried him.

Bob rose and gathering up his coat, moved towards the

door. He cast Gloria a more than speculative look. Their eyes locked and to Brian's surprise Gloria was the one that broke contact first.

"Just you be careful though. I have a feeling that long-dead skeletons are being rattled and we all know that Shakespeare's Macbeth had a bit of a point when he said it was easier to kill again, than it is to stop. So anything you dig up or think you've dug up, you give me a ring. Right?"

"Yes, Uncle Bob."

"You may be my wife's favourite niece, young lady, but potentially baiting a murderer just to have a go at your ex will not endear you to anyone."

Gloria smiled again but this time with a good deal more warmth.

"All right, all right, message received and understood."

"Just as long as it is." Bob cast her one last uneasy glance and opened the door.

Gloria remained seated and after they had gone reached for the phone. Something was making her journalistic nose twitch and not unlike a pig after truffles, she had absolutely no intention of letting it go.

Brian waited until Bob had arranged the seatbelt around his not inconsiderable girth and asked the thought uppermost in his mind.

"So she's your niece and related to pie faced ..."

"Poo breath? Good name for the little sod, although I have heard better. Yes and yes. Although strictly speaking she's the wife's niece, not mine. She's the only daughter of Moira's older sister, Eilish. She briefly married Ian Felton-Cholmondley while she was working in Fleet Street. No one from Moira's side of the family went to the wedding."

"Didn't they approve?" Brian asked, fascinated.

"Nope, just not invited. First we knew of the nuptials was seeing their picture in the Daily Mirror, taken just after the famous one was belted by the best man."

"Oh, why?"

"Apparently, our hero was discovered having carnal knowledge of a young lady, not his wife, in a linen cupboard by one of the hotel managers. The best man, however, was to put it mildly more than a bit miffed by the fact that the young lady was his sixteen-year-old daughter. Our Gloria waited until the best man had finished, pushed her beloved spouse onto a trolley containing one of those little burners they use for flambeaux, which was unfortunately still lit and walked off. After the divorce was settled and the scars had healed, she came home."

"And has been awaiting an opportunity to get even ever since?" Brian asked.

"I think the actual words were. 'I'm going to nail that bastard's balls to the wall and I hope he bleeds to death'."

"Ah."

"Exactly."

"So where do we go from here?"

"Back to Headquarters and young Duncan. You never know, he might have beginner's luck and be able to spot something we old folks have missed."

Brian chuckled and started the car. Bob looked up at the impressive facade of glass and blue metal which was the island's equivalent to Fleet Street and muttered a silent earnest prayer that if Gloria did find something, she'd at least have the good sense not to keep it to herself. Although he had a sinking feeling that she probably wouldn't.

***

Chelsea Thomas listened to the voice on the other end of the phone and after furtively checking that no one was within earshot, affirmed that Gloria had gone home. The voice paused and before he could disconnect, Chelsea used her not inconsiderable wiles to assure him that Gloria would immediately get the message. Honey dripped into the mouthpiece, rewarded by a few choice nuggets of information.

'There was no way that bitch from London was going to get a possible scoop like this,' she thought. Gathering her things she scribbled a hasty note and propped it up by the phone. Again checking that all was clear, she quietly and noiselessly hastened from the room. Once safe in her car, she made one quick call on her mobile and after arranging to meet her latest victim, she went home to change.

Gloria, returning to her desk with a cup of black coffee a few minutes later, was not best pleased to find her junior reporter not manning the phone, as promised. Michael, one of the junior newsroom reporters, sauntering back from his workstation five minutes later, found her sipping her coffee and tapping the note with frustration.

"What's up?" he asked.

"Chelsea was supposed to be holding the fort and she's just buggered off to see her sister. Some family crisis, according to this," Gloria muttered and waved the note under his nose.

"Didn't look like a crisis to me."

"What?"

"I was working down the end." He scratched his nose and narrowed his eyes before continuing, in the full and certain knowledge that Gloria was now hanging onto his every word. "The phone rings, she does her Mother Teresa impersonation, listens for about five minutes. Does a secret squirrel reccie and clears off." He paused again, before fixing her with the sharp brown eyes of a bird of prey and then threw in his ace. "Looked more like she'd got her well-polished talons into somebody else's story."

Gloria swore, her language well below gutter level and

grabbed the phone, punching digits and praying that he was still working.

Michael grinned, now totally satisfied. He had finally managed to drop that little poisonous viper Chelsea in it up to her manipulative little neck and this time Madam 'T' would hopefully give her her marching orders, or move her to reporting bunfights in the south. With any luck she'd be watching vicars buying pots of jam at the parish garden party for years to come. Happily he sauntered off, hands thrust deep in his trouser pockets and a positive swing in his step. With any luck there would still be someone left in the newsroom he could spread the good news to.

Gloria, finally making her connection, listened in growing concern as her source carefully relayed the information he had so recently given to Chelsea. Sitting back in her chair after the rather one-sided conversation had ended, she made her final decision. The number was hastily dialled before she could have second thoughts, answered on the second ring and a gruff voice barked down the line.

"Detective Inspector Bob Callow speaking, and this had better be good as it's sausage and mash night and I was on my way home."

"Uncle Bob, it's me, Gloria."

"You work fast, love. Didn't expect to hear from you until tomorrow."

"Well to be honest, ordinarily you wouldn't."

"I have a horrid feeling there is a very big 'but' coming up?"

"I was checking something, just a hunch, something that that toad Ian was allegedly involved with, a few years ago."

"And?"

"I think I may have found something."

"I'm all ears."

Gloria took a deep breath. "Some years ago Ian and a

friend from Oxford were involved in illegally obtaining certain artefacts from the Middle East, namely Egypt. Ian maintains to this day that he thought they were legally his as they had belonged to his father."

"His father?"

"Charles Cholmondley."

"Never really heard of him, which begs the question what did he do?"

"Uncle Bob, you have a nasty suspicious mind!"

"Should have been a journalist then?"

Gloria laughed.

"I say again, what did he do?" Bob asked, pulling a piece of paper towards him.

"Charles Cholmondley was an expert in some obscure branch of Middle Eastern history and at one time worked for the Egyptian government. My sources tell me that he was searching for a specific artefact or information concerning its whereabouts at about the time that he walked into the Sinai desert and didn't return."

"When was this?"

"During the late sixties; Ian must have been no more than eight or nine at the time. Although I believe that his parents actually separated when he was about two. The authorities never found the body or any reason as to why he would just wander off but ..."

"I gather we are getting to the juicy bit?"

"My sources tell me that Cholmondley senior was mixed up in some serious smuggling, fake documents, changing genuine pieces into tarty replicas."

"And how do you do that, pray?" Bob enquired with genuine interest.

"Well by all accounts it's quite easy. You first apply modern plaster and gold leaf together with some gaudy paint to your antique bust, brooch, cup or whatever it is you want to smuggle out. Then after you obtain a genuine receipt for something hideous bought in the bazaar, which has the same description, you do a swap. The garish genuine souvenir gets thrown in the Nile or nearest open fire and you get some colleague, friend or other carrier to get the 'fake' through customs as a rather loud and tasteless reminder of your stay."

"Clever. And you think Ian's beloved Papa may have either tried to cream a bit more off for himself ..." Bob mused and then thinking aloud added brightly, "or do you believe that just possibly his conscience, small as it must have been, finally bothered him?"

"Well to be frank I think that if he'd decided to go to the authorities even if it was just a quiet word at the Foreign Office, there would be at least some sort of record somewhere. No, I think on balance that the first scenario sounds about right. Ian's old man was, by all accounts, a particularly nasty piece of work, weak, spiteful and very greedy, and if he upset the wrong people at the wrong time, not particularly bright either."

"Like father like son," Bob muttered before adding the rider, "so what has this to do with me or rather the Manx constabulary?"

"Well it's a bit tenuous, I admit, but the hairs on the back of my neck are prickling. I've come up against the same name a couple of times, and it appears that he's on the Island."

"Ah." Bob exhaled a deep sigh of satisfaction: here it was, finally, a name. Something he could get his teeth into, unless of course it was his corpse.

"Samuel Lawrence, the historian. He was working with Ian's father for a brief time in Cairo. He is at present on the Island working on the filming of the Glashton. In fact, it was his original idea and he knew your body."

"What?" Bob almost shrieked with relief. At long last, a live suspect!

"According to my old editor, your cadaver is one Barney Goldsmith, a freelance investigative journalist. He was working on a story about the theft of Middle Eastern art and was on his way over here, to interview Mr Lawrence."

"And your source is certain about this?"

"Very much so, as he was forking out for the advance. He thought I'd like to know as young Barney was particularly interested in Ian's foray into this rather murky underworld and my old lunch partner wanted to know if I had any further dirt."

"Charming people you mix with."

"Any use?"

"Oh yes, if your source is right I think we may pay Mr Lawrence a visit."

"There may be a bit of a problem," Gloria stated, her voice growing more than slightly cagey. Bob catching the tone, frowned into his mouthpiece.

"Why do I have the distinct feeling that the bad news is coming?"

"Mr Lawrence may already know about my enquiries."

"Oh?" Bob gave a throaty growl of disapproval. The sort of sound a big cat would make if suddenly deprived of its dinner.

"Chelsea, a very junior reporter and soon to be ex-member of staff, took the original phone call from my source and on the pretext of sorting out a domestic problem has cleared off," Gloria announced angrily.

"I gather from your furious tone of voice that you are worried about her?"

"Yes," Gloria bluntly replied. "These people, the ones that may or may not be involved with my ex, his father, Sam Lawrence and young Barney Goldsmith, are not saints. If the death of Mr Goldsmith is their work, then the little idiot may already be in some considerable danger. Uncle Bob, we are talking about a lot of money, probably an obscene sum of money and the sort of skeletons you would hide wardrobes in, rather than the other way around."

"The kind of mess that you don't touch without the entire Swat team and the collective might of the fraud squad, customs and excise and anyone else with either a firearms licence or a black belt in Judo?"

"Exactly."

"And how long has this nosy young lady been gone?"

"About half an hour."

"You wait there. I'll be round in ten minutes with the car. You ring her home and then you ring Mr Lawrence and after I've picked you up we'll pay both of them a visit they are unlikely to forget in a hurry."

Bob put the phone down and calling loudly for Duncan, who was in the pleasant process of chatting up a young WPC in the corridor, grabbed his car keys and left Police Headquarters at a mild trot.

***

Brian climbed the stairs to his flat and leant against the wall of the poorly-lit corridor before inserting the key in the lock. He was not looking forward to the coming meal. Normally the thought of Caroline, a tall glass of wine, his favourite restaurant and a few hours of peace would have been heavenly but shared as they would be by his estranged father ... Brian mentally shook himself and girded his loins. Well he had to get it over with at some time, so he might as well get on with it.

Brian opened the door and plunged into the room, not with some classical Latin quote as was his usual habit when being forced into doing something he didn't want to, but with the words "Doh, I really don't want to do this." Caroline looked up from her quiet task of painting her nails the colour of fresh blood and regarded him from under long mascara-coated black lashes.

"You sound like Homer Simpson!" she announced, screwing the top back onto the small glass bottle of nail polish. "On balance I think I'd prefer you to grow up as Uncle Bob."

Brian chuckled. "I'll hold you to that," he laughed, bending to kiss the soft skin of her cheek. She had done something to her hair, it was, he thought almost a completely different colour, in fact hadn't she been blonde this morning?

"Your hair?" he queried, beginning to flounder.

"Do you like it?" Caroline asked, preening.

"Er ..." Brian had the sudden instinctive feeling, that to tread carefully at this particular point might make a difference to his lifespan. "Yes, it's different." And then on seeing her facial muscles tighten added hastily. "It suits you." Caroline gave him a long, love-filled look, which if it had come from anyone else would have had him running for the hills, and stood up.

"I knew you would love it, once you got used to it," she announced.

He was just making a tactical withdrawal to the bedroom to change, when she dropped the bombshell.

"Oh and by the way your father rang earlier. He said was it all right with us if he brought his new girlfriend? I said it would be OK." Brian stood in the doorway completely immobile.

"Brian love, I can ring him back and ..."

Brian physically pulled himself together and shook his head. "No, it's fine. I'm fine. It's his life after all and if he prefers to lead it with some twenty-something airhead, instead of his intelligent wife of twenty-five years then who am I to quibble? I mean to say if he wishes to discuss our wedding with some complete stranger!" Words suddenly failing and his voice husky with violently suppressed anger, he fled to the bedroom and slammed the door.

Caroline stood and stared at the back of the white-glossed door and heaved a heavy heartfelt sigh. Now was possibly not the right time to tell him her other bit of news.

***

Firmly she held his hand as they marched into Ciappelli's restaurant. Crisp white linen tablecloths covered variously sized round tables. Candles glowed amongst the silver plates and highly polished glasses and directly in front of them Brian's father stood nervously and carefully cleared his throat. Caroline started because the physical resemblance between father and son was almost uncanny. They both, she thought now that she saw them together, looked almost exactly like Brian Blessed, the actor. With the possible exception of the fact that Brian's father had a grey grizzled beard and Brian was scrupulously clean-shaven.

"Er, hello son, I'd like you to meet my secretary Edna and soon to be the second Mrs Clague."

Brian swallowed and turned to face the woman half-hidden in the shadows. Brian looked at her and she at him and then with relief almost palpable, he smiled down at her, baring nearly all his teeth.

Caroline, following behind, stared from one to the other and feigning a sudden fit of noisy coughing, smothered her laughter in a hastily-grabbed bundle of paper tissues.

"Well, now that everyone has met, let's have something to eat, eh son? You must be hungry. My son," he informed Edna, holding her tiny hand in his, "is a policeman, a detective."

Surprised, Brian sat and watched him. He had never before heard that degree of open pride in his father's voice and with a slight shock, began to wonder if he'd ever really known him at all.

Throughout the long and to his continued astonishment, pleasant meal, Brian observed and mentally noted. Edna, far from being the imagined golddigger, turned out to be a mousy-haired widow of uncertain years with two teenage children. Her husband had worked on the building of bridges for aid workers in various parts of the world. Until that is, the one he was working on was blown up by some obscure but violent radical group of terrorists. Even Brian felt sorry for her as she briefly related her life history up until the point when she had turned up at his father's office in her capacity as the latest in a long line of temporary secretaries. They had hit it off from the moment she had brought him a drinkable cup of tea with real milk, and a perfectly typed letter.

They were just discussing the price of wedding cars and the average cost per head of a decent wedding lunch when the Maitre D whispered a few hurried words to Brian as he arrived at their table with a waitress bearing a second round of special coffees. Hastily, Brian pressed his lips to his napkin and moved swiftly to the waiting phone.

Slowly he returned and at a concerned look from Caroline, announced,

"That was Duncan, there may have been another attack. He's sending a car round now. I'm really sorry, love." Caroline looked up at him and shook her head fondly.

"Not your fault, is it? Go on, I'll settle things here, you just get out there and as Bob would say 'Catch the bugger and throw away the key'." Brian leant down and locked his lips with hers, before exiting at almost a run.

"And now you know why this place is his favourite

restaurant," she announced, taking a slow sip of heavily alcohol-laced coffee, the cream tickling her nose.

"The superb food and wonderful wine?" Gerald Clague answered, carefully unwrapping a dark chocolate mint.

"No."

"The service and delightful surroundings?" Edna asked, smiling.

"No."

"We give up then," Gerald announced, popping the mint into his mouth.

"It's five minutes away from Police Headquarters," Caroline informed them, as watching from the window, she saw the white striped police car squeal to a halt, pick Brian up and then with blue light flashing, scorch its way back into the gathering darkness.

***

Chelsea sipped her wine and glanced seductively, with what she had once been told was her Princess Diana look, at the man sitting opposite. She knew exactly what she was doing and had left almost nothing out of her story. And there he sat, rubbing his finger around the neck of the glass, his smile that of barely suppressed lust.

She had her scoop. He would for a small sum, as yet unnegotiated, spill the beans and dish so much dirt that they'd need to disinfect the entire newsroom afterwards.

It was as she turned her head to refill her glass, that he hit her.

Afterwards, when she regained an almost dreamlike consciousness, she could smell and taste the sea. Hard slate lay beneath her and above, a weight pressed her down. She was being kissed, a tongue forced into her mouth, as a long pulsating hardness was forced between her legs. She began to push him away, anger coursed through her.

This was not what she'd intended, not what she wanted and it hurt. Rock cut into her back and she tore at him, now frantic to get away. He was heavy and strong and she knew, beginning to really enjoy himself. Her back ached and stung as he thrust in and out, her screams now stifled by the hand over her mouth. She bit it, hard. The thrusting grew fiercer, as he forced her legs further apart; the hand was momentarily moved and replaced with the other wearing a leather glove, impossible to bite.

Finally with one last shuddering push he seemed to have finished. Chelsea lay quiet, hoping that would be it. He stood up and looked down on her. He'd enjoyed that.

She'd been good, young and soft. Chelsea tried to sit up, her shoulders ached, her breasts bruised and scratched, her nails torn where she'd tried to defend herself. Ruefully, she rubbed at the dark marks on her wrists and then at the bruises on her neck. Date rape, she thought bitterly, he'd say she'd asked for it. He'd say that she'd thrown herself at him. Hotly she remembered the wine and the short, deliberately provocative outfit. A mounting anger, mostly directed at her self, filled her head.

Suddenly he bent towards her, scooping her up in strong arms and without warning, half threw, half dropped her into the freezing dark water lapping around the rock. Chelsea gasped, the cold hitting her as the sea caught and held her in its grip. Hands closed around her as she struggled to stand on the moving pebbles and shale beneath her bare feet.

Fighting both the cold water and her assailant she managed to scream before she was forced back under the water and the bitter salt invaded her mouth and lungs. Shouts sounded above the water, as a couple walking their dog rushed to her aid.

She lay unseeing, unfeeling as they pulled her from the waves and carefully laid her on the sharp stones. The dog snuffled at her as the sounds of sirens pulsated in the evening air. Chelsea slept as one dead, her brain deprived of oxygen for one second too long. Her assailant, safe amongst the darkness of rocks and water, threw back his head and silently laughed.

***

Chelsea's landlady stood, arms crossed, legs bowed and refused to let either Bob or Gloria past until she was more than convinced that they were exactly who they said they were.

"Anyway you won't catch her now, gone out she has and won't be back 'til morning either."

"Oh, and why do you say that?" Bob enquired.

"She was wearing the sort of things they'd have arrested you for a couple of years ago. That's why. Hardly worth bothering to dress in what she had on." The landlady sniffed.

"Short skirt, tight blouse, that sort of thing?" Gloria enquired icily, well aware that the landlady had given her outfit a more than disapproving look when she'd walked in behind her uncle.

"Skirt? it was more of a belt! Made that get up of yours look like a nun's habit!"

"Really? What exactly was she dressed in?" Bob asked, quietly extracting his notepad from the voluminous folds of his old fawn-coloured mac. It had once been a smart Burberry but had definitely seen better days. Brian referred to it, almost affectionately, as Bob's Columbo outfit.

"One of them tight fitting tops, that look like the top of someone's petticoat. A black skirt that hardly covered her backside. Fishnet stockings and before you ask, I know they was stockings 'cause you could see the tops. Pair of high-heeled red shoes and one of them little fake fur jackets in a sort of coffee colour. God knows how she managed to change that quick because she was in and out in minutes, well ten maybe."

"I don't suppose she said where she was going?" Bob enquired.

"Didn't say but she had a man waiting for her."

"Did you see him then?"

"What? Oh no, he wasn't waiting here for her but stands to reason she wouldn't have dressed like that, just for a night out with the girls."

"Right. Don't suppose you know how she left – own car, walking?"

Bob was about to put the notebook back and fish for his car keys when she said, "Walking in those shoes! Took a taxi, didn't she. That's what made me come into the hall. It were out there blowing its horn! I was about to go out and give him a piece of my mind, when she swans down the stairs reeking of perfume and looking like something the cat wouldn't even spit at."

"I don't suppose you can remember which cab company it was?"

"Nope, but it were one of them black London taxis."

"Great. Shouldn't be too difficult to trace then. Thanks very much for your help." Bob smiled a delighted smile and moved towards the door. Gloria, following in his wake, turned and taking in at a glance the old Victorian staircase and hall, paint peeling and paper curling in blisters from the wall, shuddered.

Outside in the fresh air Bob leant against the car while he dialled Headquarters on his mobile and desperately hoped that young Duncan had found the address for Samuel Lawrence.

It was while Gloria was driving towards Laxey that the mobile bleeped and burped beside him.

"Yes," he barked into the small plastic rectangle.

"Bob?"

"Tavistock?" Bob surprised, made slowing motions to Gloria, who slowed down, parking on the kerb, hazard lights flashing.

"Has something happened?"

"Why?"

"I was in the bath reading those notes over again, when the room went dark. I could feel someone pushing me down into the water, it was very cold and I really hurt, inside, outside, everywhere. Then I heard people running and saw lights flashing. Bob, something's out there hiding in the rocks and laughing at us. Please tell me it's all a bad case of alcoholic poisoning and too many videos of the X Files?"

Bob sighed deeply. He had an uneasy feeling that Samuel Lawrence would have to wait.

"Tavistock can you remember anything else? Did you see anything else? Anything at all?"

"Well, yes."

"What?"

"A high-heeled red shoe."

"Oh God."

"Bob?"

"Nothing, thanks for ringing. It wasn't a dream, a nightmare maybe and somebody else's at that. I have to go. I'll see you tomorrow."

Bob disconnected and immediately redialled Duncan.

"Duncan lad, don't ask any questions, just listen. Get hold of the lads in the incident room see if anyone's reported some sort of disturbance anywhere on any of the Island's beaches. Yes – now. Good lad. Yes, I'll wait."

Gloria sat twisting the large ruby ring round and round her middle finger, again and again until the skin showed raw against the gold band. Bob drummed his fingers on the dashboard and stared out into the gathering gloom.

Mist curled across the road and birds sang deep in the woods on either side of the parked car.

They both started as the mobile buzzed between them. Bob reached for it almost reluctantly. He listened in silence.

"Right lad, get down to the hospital and wait. Dig out Brian too ... What? I don't care if he's having dinner with the Chief Minister himself, just get him ... I'm on my way." He glared down at the gently glowing display and switched the mobile off.

"They think they may have found your colleague." Gloria sighed and began to smile.

"Not so fast, lass. It's not good news. A young lady was seen struggling with an unknown assailant, wearing some sort of mask. They've taken her to Nobles. Thing is the medics say she's been very badly assaulted, possibly raped and they suspect that she's also taken a severe blow to the head. At present she's stable but comatose. They don't hold out much hope of recovery but it's early days." Gloria sat, stunned, as the news slowly filtered through.

"Bob."

"Yes lass?"

"If Chelsea hadn't taken that call and I'd gone haring off, that could have been me."

"Yes, I know. That thought had already occurred to your old Uncle Bob. You all right to drive?"

Gloria nodded and started the engine, desperately glad that she had something useful to do.

"Only I think we need to get back to Douglas and positively see whether this unlucky young lady is really your erstwhile colleague."

Later they sat in Bob's front lounge. Moira held Gloria in her arms for the first time in years, as Gloria sobbed uncontrollably. Bob drank hot milky coffee, laced with about an inch of brandy and closed his eyes.

Chelsea Thomas had been quietly declared dead at 2.31 a.m. She had never regained consciousness.

Chapter 8

Bob sat in the car outside Samuel Lawrence's rented holiday accommodation and went through his notes with Brian and Duncan. Bob suspected it would take his niece some time to come to terms with Chelsea's death. More so because as Gloria had herself admitted, over their third cup of brandy with a splash of coffee, she had never really liked her.

Guilt was a terrible thing but he suspected that if the rest of the newsroom felt the same, it would at least keep the investigation in the forefront of news and editorial comment for some time to come. And now he had to interview his prime and so far only suspect. Brian had thoughtfully relayed as much of his previous conversation with Mr Lawrence as he could remember. One glaring anomaly had hit them both as they compared notes and that was that he'd denied any knowledge of knowing Barney Goldsmith. Which, according to Gloria's source, was completely untrue.

Taking a deep breath, Bob left the warm muggy confines of the car for the bracing air outside. Brian sent up a quiet prayer that Samuel Lawrence didn't smoke indoors and Duncan wondered if there was any hope of getting something to eat at any point in the near future.

Samuel Lawrence stood to one side of the carefully pleated net curtains and pondered. He'd been briefed already as to what he should and should not say to the steadily advancing policemen. The two youngsters would be easy but the older one would be more difficult. He had a feeling that Bob Callow had the sort of terrier-like qualities that petty criminals such as himself found most difficult to out-manoeuvre. He would have to be very careful. He might even have to tell a few small truths. His bags, already packed, sat in a dark corner of the wardrobe. With any luck the interrogation would only take half an hour or so and then he could depart hastily to the airport and eventually a small comfortable canal barge, which would, hopefully, be somewhat difficult to track. And if the police couldn't find him, *they* wouldn't be able to either.

His train of thought stopped abruptly with the ring of the doorbell and composing his features, he moved to let the police in.

Bob, his eyes roving about the room, finally let them fall on a pile of books leaning drunkenly against a green upholstered armchair.

"Still keeping up on local legends then?" he enquired, his face a picture of studied innocence. Samuel, momentarily off his guard, nodded.

"I believe it was your idea to film the story of the Glashton," Bob remarked, picking one of the leather-bound books up and flicking through the worn, yellowing pages.

"Why the Isle of Man?" Bob enquired, this time fixing his prey with a steely stare.

"Why not?" Samuel shrugged and sat down on the nearest chair. Duncan moved towards the doorway and quietly hovered. After a few minutes he carefully left the room and with almost feline stealth, explored the rest of the flat.

Samuel, seated with his back to the open door, was blissfully unaware of Duncan's foray. He was more worried about Bob Callow than he was prepared to admit, even to himself.

"So, what may I do for the Manx Constabulary?" Samuel asked, his tone light and mildly bantering.

Bob watched him for a few brief moments, sensing the uneasiness behind the forced jocularity.

"Well. We could start with a few mild lies and then maybe, after the application of thumbscrews, you could tell us the truth," Bob replied, leaning against the mantelpiece, which was sparsely adorned with a cracked ornamental china dog and a large pot of plastic ivy. The small variegated leaves were dusty and yellow with neglect.

"I have absolutely no idea what you mean, officer."

"Really?"

"I'm sure I would never willingly lie to the officers of the law. After all, what have I got to lie about?"

"What indeed?" Brian murmured sarcastically as he tentatively sat down upon a small, Dralon-covered sofa. Samuel Lawrence gave him a quick, surprised look.

"One of my colleagues tells me that you have no idea who our recent body on the beach was?" Bob commented.

"That's right."

"Even though, according to WPC Skillicorn, she spent some time in your trailer yesterday, showing you some easily recognisable photographs of young Mr Goldsmith?"

"Goldsmith, was that his name? I had no idea." Samuel nervously rubbed the palms of his hands together and tried to meet Bob's limpid gaze.

"Really? Then it wasn't Mr Barney Goldsmith that you were seen dining with in a small select Soho wine bar, last Friday?"

Samuel gave a small start of surprise and a nervous tic appeared at the corner of his left eye. It pulsed gently and

Samuel pushed his glasses up against the bridge of his nose in the vain attempt to hide it with the tortoiseshell-coloured frame.

"Oh, and where exactly did you get this wholly imaginative piece of information from?"

"Reginald Michael, your old bridge partner and editor of one of Fleet Street's less noble rags."

"Reginald. Well, old love, I'm afraid, dear old Reginald must be mistaken. Not about me of course, after all, we were at school together but about my companion. Dear old Reg, I keep telling him he needs new lenses in those ghastly NHS specs of his." Samuel laughed at his own joke rather too heartily and in the stony silence that followed gazed selfconsciously at the carpet.

"Mr Michael has confirmed that the young man was indeed Mr Barney Goldsmith and is quite happy to go into court and swear to Mr Goldsmith's identity."

"He's mistaken."

"I don't think one could mistake one's own stepson but we can always wait until Mr Michael arrives on the Island with his current wife for the formal identification."

Brian had never seen anyone poleaxed before but he couldn't help thinking that that particular phrase was the only one that could currently apply to the expression on the elderly historian's face.

"Oh ..."

"Oh. Indeed."

"So now that we both know that you and Mr Goldsmith not only met but spent several hours in deep and meaningful discussions, over a couple of bottles of Pinot Grigio perhaps we could dispense with the usual porkies and get down to a bit of truth?"

"Or what?"

"Or, I can arrest you for the murders of Barney Goldmith and Chelsea Thomas."

"What?" Samuel Lawrence shouted.

"Well, you see, we don't have anyone else in the frame and as you appear to be our one and only link and we don't want to have to waste any more of the taxpayers' hard-earned revenue …"

"You can't be serious?"

"Oh but I am. Perfectly serious."

"But I don't know any Chelsea Thomas!"

Bob moved towards him and leaning forwards, he almost thrust his face into that of Mr Lawrence's.

"Chelsea Thomas rang your number from her bedsit yesterday and we have the Manx Telecom information to prove it. The call lasted five and a half minutes. We also have a statement from the driver of a local taxi firm who will swear on oath that he picked her up from her home yesterday evening and deposited her at this address. Somebody, according to our friendly cabby, let her in to this flat at approximately 7.30 p.m. And at 9.15 p.m she was being rushed to Nobles Hospital where she later died."

"Good God!"

"You are, as Ann Robinson would say, the weakest link and as such should be cautioned and banged up to await the Second Deemster's pleasure," Bob remarked, his voice dripping ice.

"Look, I can see how it must appear, really I do but it wasn't me."

"Then who was it?"

"I can't …" Samuel Lawrence looked from one to the other and then to their intense astonishment, burst into tears.

"It wasn't me, it wasn't."

"Then who was it?" Bob asked, handing him a large, mangled, white cotton handkerchief.

Samuel blew his nose and wiped the last of the tears from his eyes.

"All right. I admit I met Barney in Soho. He wanted some information on Ian Felton-Cholmondley."

"What precisely?"

"His smuggling days. I told him what I knew about his father. We met, you see, in Cairo years ago. He was searching for certain artefacts."

"What artefacts?"

"I can't remember precisely what …"

Bob glared at him.

Samuel Lawrence gulped back a sob and blew his nose noisily and wetly into the handkerchief. Bob made a mental note not to ask for it back, and glared at his quarry even more ferociously.

"Documents, a letter written by St Paul to one of the other apostles."

"What about?"

"I don't know, he said that he had half and that the other half was in a museum in Berlin. I don't know what it was that he found. I do know that he was excited and planned to see the other half of the letter."

"Did he say which museum?"

"No, I got the distinct impression there was something dodgy about it."

"A private museum?" Bob asked.

Samuel lifted his head and fixed Bob with a brief surprised look before returning to his contemplation of the grimy cigarette-burnt brown carpet.

"Possibly. Whatever it was, it was very valuable, priceless in fact."

"Did he ever find it?"

"I don't think so. I left to come back to England and Charles disappeared shortly afterwards. But his papers and all his private notes he passed on to his son."

"And how do you know that?"

"Because he sent them to me with a note that Ian was to

get them when he came of age."

"Why you?"

"I don't know."

Bob sensed the direct lie but let it pass.

"So what did you tell Mr Goldsmith?" he asked, studying his own dust- encrusted fingertips.

"I showed him copies of the letter and the other documents. He had information about Sir Arthur Felton, he thought that Charles died because of work that Sir Arthur was involved in during the war. I told him that was utter rubbish. I told that lady reporter the same thing. She left here about fifteen minutes after she arrived. I don't know what happened to her – she said she had to meet someone."

"I see."

"Now do you believe me?"

"No, not entirely. Which is why you will accompany us to the station where we will need to take certain samples of bodily fluids, just to rule you out of our enquiries. And while you are waiting you may decide to tell me the truth. I don't suppose you still have copies of the papers Charles Cholmondley sent you?"

"Yes. You can find them in that drawer there. Though much good may they do you."

Samuel Lawrence rose, and opening the drawer he'd pointed to, removed a roll of papers tied with an old length of threadbare blue ribbon.

Bob held them in his hands and then looked deep into Samuel's eyes.

"You may not have had anything to do with either the death of Mr Goldsmith or Miss Thomas but if someone else dies because you've withheld evidence of any sort then I will hold you directly responsible. Do I make myself abundantly plain?"

"Yes."

"Good. Brian, I would like you to formerly caution Mr Lawrence and then you can escort him to the car. Duncan, you can drive."

Duncan, reappearing in the doorway, grinned and opened the front door.

Duncan and Bob stood like attendants at a funeral as Brian read Samuel Lawrence his rights. As the words 'murder' and 'rape' were spoken in the dusty silence, Samuel Lawrence trembled and a second nervous tic began to beat quietly just below the lank hair falling across his temple.

"I think," Bob muttered looking at the expanse of blue sky above him, "that I need a bit of air."

Duncan and Brian exchanged puzzled glances as they bundled their chief suspect unceremoniously into the back of the car and after a moment's hesitation, drove off, leaving Bob to his thoughts. Bob watched them until they disppeared from view behind a row of Victorian cottages and then phoned Tavistock on his mobile.

"Tavistock I need a lift. Pick me up at the end of the beach down in Old Laxey and bring some coffee." Cutting her off before any comments could be made, Bob began the long walk down to the shore, every line on his face creased in thought.

***

It was some thirty minutes later that Tavistock finally found him, sitting not unlike a large middle-aged gnome in the centre of an off-white, paint-encrusted, concrete bollard. He was watching a group of barely clad youngsters trying to push what looked like a tractor tyre into the foaming waves. Shrieking with excitement, they managed to manhandle it out far enough into the water to allow them to scramble precariously onto its black glossy top.

It floated none too steadily in the gently pulsating surf, as one by one the clinging bodies fell or were pushed off.

"So why did you want to see me?" Tavistock asked.

Bob, startled by her appearance, turned towards her. "Why is it that you always manage to sneak up on me?" Bob moaned crossly.

"Because I'm a mum. Mums have to sneak around otherwise they'd never know what their delightful offspring were doing."

"I'm a dad and I don't sneak?"

"Dad's don't have to. Besides, most fathers haven't a clue what their children are doing and to be honest wouldn't care much if they did," Tavistock observed, watching as one child hurled himself at the tyre, which bucked wildly and deposited him into the centre of a large, white-fringed wave.

"Aren't they cold?" she muttered, pulling her cardigan around her. It was her favourite large fluffy cardigan with a huge picture of a panda on the back. Richard hated it and so it only got an airing when he wasn't around.

"They should be, shouldn't they?" Bob agreed with a smile. "I mean to say it's barely July and there they are immersing themselves in large unwarmed portions of the Irish Sea. But they're kids and let's face it, enjoying themselves, so who the hell cares?" he replied with a shrug as he remembered not dissimilar incidents in his own childhood.

"Come on," he said, moving down towards the water's edge.

"What are you doing?" Tavistock asked, as Bob suddenly bent down and in a hunched position began to remove his socks and shoes.

"I feel a paddle coming on," Bob answered, looking up at her with a wicked grin.

"You're mad!"

"Probably. You coming or what?" he asked, rolling up his trousers and advancing towards the incoming tide.

Tavistock laughed despite her determination to remain coldly aloof and removed her own sandals. Together they wandered away from the children towards the quiet end of the rock-fringed beach. Trees bent towards them, their branches bowed down with the lushness of summer foliage. Light winked and blinked above them as the summer sun pushed through the leaves. Warm air scurried across the gold, shell-speckled sand, caressing their bare toes as it passed. They walked in companionable silence for some time before finding a large slab of rock cooking gently under the afternoon sun. Tavistock sank down onto its hot surface and stretched, cat-like.

Bob, seating himself next to her, gathered a variety of pebbles and intermittently threw them into the hesitantly approaching surf. Mannanan, sheltering from the heat, watched them from the depths of the surrounding wood and held his peace.

"This is nice," Tavistock observed. "It's actually quite warm out of the wind."

"Yep. Be better if we had a spot of something," Bob said, looking hungrily at the large bag she still had slung over her shoulder.

"You mean a nice cup of milky coffee and some of my mother's coffee and walnut cake? Well as it happens ..." Tavistock grinned and produced a flask, two plastic cups and a large square-shaped slab of tin foil.

"You are a star!" Bob cried eagerly, unwrapping the package that contained several pre-cut slices of a gooey coffee-coloured cake, sandwiched lavishly with honey-coloured buttercream.

"So what can I do to help?" Tavistock asked as they sat side by side alternately sipping and munching.

"I have a bit of a problem," Bob admitted.

"Only a bit of one?"

"You can laugh!" Bob grumbled. "I've been up half the night dealing with journalists, one of whom managed to get herself raped and then murdered. We do have a suspect who says he didn't do it."

"They always say that!"

"True. Thing is, I have that odd thumb-pricking feeling that lurking around is something really nasty. Too nasty to be the doings of some elderly seedy historian."

"And just which elderly historian are we discussing?" Tavistock asked.

"Bloke by the name of Samuel Lawrence."

"Sam the Spam, bent as the proverbial corkscrew, Lawrence."

"That's the one!"

"But he's gay. Everyone knows that he was a legend in his own lunchtime for the number of conquests he made in the world of fringe theatre and that was before it was legal."

"Blatant?"

"He had an Ann Summers party a couple of years ago!"

"What's wrong with that?"

"Men only?"

"Ah."

"Ah indeed. He likes women, don't get me wrong, and he's frankly one of the best listeners I've ever come across when it comes to tales of woe and sorrow from both sexes but I'd say he'd be absolutely the last one on my list for female rape. I'm assuming it was a she."

"You assume right."

"So?"

"He fits the bill. I have a witness who deposited the girl at his flat. I have another witness who says he saw them walking down towards the beach. And I have definite links between him and our first body. I know he has had something to do with both murders which he hotly denies and yet ..."

"What?"

"Dunno – sounds weird."

"The mad druid was weird."

"No, he was just your average everyday mad axe-murderer. This is different, this smells all wrong."

"Ah. So what can I do?"

"Have a look at these papers." Bob handed over the sheaf of closely written documents and Tavistock squinted at them despairingly.

"And I thought it was just doctors who couldn't write in legible joined-up writing. This guy hadn't even mastered rudimentary block capitals. Good grief, what on earth is that?"

"Looks like a picture of a dog with an eagle on his head having a ..."

"Could be an ink blot?" Tavistock added hastily before Bob could get into his stride. Bob chuckled and sipped his coffee.

Tavistock shook her head; she couldn't make head nor tail of the closely written script and one of the papers, which looked as though it had been torn from a book of some sort, was also charred around the edges. Tavistock waved the pages in front of Bob's face before setting them carefully back onto the rock between them.

"Anything?" Bob asked.

"Nope."

"Perhaps you need help?" Mannanan interjected. Bob groaned as theatrically as possible and Tavistock laughed.

"How did you know we were here?" Bob moaned.

"I have my sources," Mannanan replied a little smugly as he settled himself down beside Tavistock.

"How do you mean?" Bob and Tavistock asked in

perfect unison.

"I eavesdropped on your telephone conversation."

"Oh."

"So what is it you need to find out?" Mannanan gently enquired.

"I'd like to know what these papers are all about, as everybody who seems to know anything about them is either dead or has clammed up tighter than a Manx Queenie," Bob replied.

"Hum ..." Mannanan placed his hand on the letters and sighed. He closed his eyes and sat deep in thought for a few minutes. When he opened them again he looked at them oddly and Bob had the distinct impression that he was toying with the idea of not telling them anything at all.

"Look, eventually I or somebody else is going to find out what's going on, in the meantime if you don't help us somebody else will also be lying in the mortuary with a sheet over their face surrounded by sobbing parents making funeral arrangements instead of the wedding they'd planned."

"Wedding?" Tavistock asked.

"Brian rang just before you arrived. Chelsea Thomas, the young lady who got too close to these wretched things was going to get married on Saturday to a young lad from Ramsey. He's doing some sort of hotel management training at the Mount Murray. He was in the throws of sorting out his own reception when her parents rang him. Not a happy bunny by all accounts."

"Well she should have thought of that before she went around sticking her nose in things that were none of her business," Mannanan muttered.

"How can you say that?" Tavistock, plainly horrified, rounded on him.

"Because it's true."

Tavistock glared at him. Bob, by now seething with curiosity, watched him with a face of studied bland indifference.

"So care to let us in on the big secret?"

"I suppose I don't have much choice," Mannanan muttered.

"Not much," Bob agreed.

"Tavistock, hold the letters and let me place my hands on yours."

"Do we need a third person like we did in Manchester?" Bob asked, quietly wondering to himself which unlucky sod he could rope in.

"No, not this time. Tavistock will see what she is able to and then will tell you all about it, she just needs my help to translate emotions into memories."

"Right," Bob agreed, hoping it would all make sense afterwards.

Tavistock picked up the bundle of papers and gingerly held them. Mannanan placed his hands on hers and nothing happened.

"Well?" Bob asked.

"Well what?" Tavistock snapped back.

Tavistock was on the point of verbally clipping Bob around the ears when she spotted two distant figures walking towards them across the sand.

"Shh!" she said. "Someone's coming."

Bob looked to where she was staring and saw a plastic bag rolling towards the white, froth-rimmed waves.

It was the solid wall of heat hitting her in the face that made her realise that the two figures walking towards her were anywhere but in the Isle of Man. As they approached, their forms expanding and retracting in the shimmering haze, she had an immediate impression of towering red rock, sand and isolation. They were arguing, their voices harsh and guttural. One turned and began to walk away, then the other threw something that looked to Tavistock like some sort of bolas. There was a moment when nothing happened followed by a sickening sound of bones being smashed and the man who had walked away fell to the ground. His body lay crumpled on the ground as the other searched pockets and the rough folds and seams of his jacket. Finally finding nothing, the man dropped to his knees and screamed upwards towards the encircling birds of prey. A scream of such hopeless desolation that Tavistock covered her ears and closed her eyes to cut out the sights and sounds of a death which now appeared utterly pointless.

When she opened them again the heat was beginning to fade, clouds hung high above red cliffs of wind-carved stone. Sand blew in eddies of broken light across her feet. A man was sitting beside her on the rock and in front of him another bearded Arab gentleman paced.

"And so the trail goes cold, my friend. So we will try another road." The man on the rock sighed and extracting a long wooden pipe, began to fiddle with tobacco and flame until a soft curl of aromatic smoke rose heavenwards.

"I was so sure that they would have brought it here," the other replied, shrugging his shoulders.

"My dear Absolam, the ways of the early Christians are strange even to me and I understand them better than you, I think?"

"And what does that inner voice tell you?"

"My inner voice urges me to travel back towards the remnants of empire. The exchange must have been made here, the letter leads us to believe that but I don't believe it was kept here. This place is too well known. The Romans would have marched an army in to claim it and your race, my friend, would have destroyed it."

"Yes, I rather think they would."

"So we return to civilisation tomorrow. We take a train

to the coast and from there a boat to Rome. Then we follow our protector to Ireland. We know he went there and somehow either hid the thing en route or he found a safer place amongst the monasteries and abbeys he later visited. Either way there is nothing more to do here. Come, we had better hurry, I can almost feel the brown shirts sniffing at my heels and the dogs of war are held back with a thinning leash."

"He is not strong enough yet, surely?"

"He has the politicians in his hand and now that the army has fallen in with his plans, who knows. On balance I think the sooner we reach the relative safety of what they call the Emerald Isle the better."

"I will ready the horses, Professor Bergman."

The professor continued to sit, puffing gently into the stem of his smoking pipe, as his companion wandered away into the darkening air.

Tavistock blinked quickly as a breath of wind heavily laden with sand stung her cheeks. The rocks faded and the air cooled as the light of a summer's day returned together with the ordinary sights and scents of a Manx beach.

***

Sir Arthur studied their faces and let out a long drawn out sigh.

"Perhaps you had better come in before the reporter who is hiding in that tree ... No please don't look, it will only encourage the little blighter. Besides," he added thoughtfully, old eyes sparkling with wickedness, "I thought I might just get some old crow-frighteners out, we used to call them cherry bangers."

"Cherry bangers?" Duncan asked, perplexed.

"I see you haven't lived in the country, officer. A cherry banger is a small explosive device, which frightens birds out of their skulls and hopefully stops them nibbling the buds off cherry trees. Otherwise there would at times be little or no harvest. Doubtless the gooey-eyed animal rights activist has already banned the things but I doubt that even they would consider journalists to be an endangered species."

Duncan considered the criminal aspect of the case and coming to the conclusion that as the reporter was trespassing on private property it was a case of two wrongs making a very large splash on the front page, nervously looked to Brian for support.

Brian, who had by then had more than enough of anyone even vaguely connected with the press, at any level, muttered, "Vermin control," in dark undertones and hastily pushed Duncan into the cool shadows of the hall. Sir Arthur carefully closed the door after them and turning to the phone on a small walnut table flanking the wall, quietly punched a few numbers. He waited patiently for a connection to be made and then hoarsely muttered, "Chocks away."

With shaking freckle-flecked fingers he replaced the phone, and motioning them to be silent by holding one finger against his mouth, he sidled around to the side of a door left ajar. All three cautiously moved towards the net curtains hanging almost to the floor in the small room adjacent to the front door. They could, from there, clearly see the large beech tree shading the end of the drive and perched in it a green and brown-clad figure, clutching a black plastic box.

They waited.

Nothing happened.

Rooks settled in the other trees across the drive.

Somewhere in the distance a tractor panted across a field and deep in the folds of Brian's pocket a mobile whirred.

"Oh ..." Brian muttered, extracting and answering it.

"Who is it?"

There was a pause as he listened. The figure in the tree shuffled uneasily.

"I'll ring you back."

Carefully he switched it off and replaced it back into the inside pocket of his jacket. He hadn't disconnected it entirely but had turned the volume down so low, it could still be heard but not unless you really listened.

"Who was that?" Duncan asked.

"Uncle Bob. Wanted me to know he thought he had a lead and how was I doing. Then he said he'd be available later when he'd seen someone."

"Oh." Duncan, straining his eyes, peered at the tree, sensing the tension emanating from Sir Arthur they had little doubt that something was about to happen.

There was a flash of grey smoke, an explosion of sound and something large crashed down through the branches.

Sir Arthur, chuckling gleefully, rubbed his hands together and almost bounced from the room.

All three marched from the house. This, thought Duncan, was better than grouse shooting.

From behind the wall surrounding the house and directly behind the tree came voices. One loud and almost hysterical, the other growling in tones they all knew only too well. Sir Arthur muttered 'Oops' and began to sidle off, thoughts of where to go to escape fleeing quickly as Brian and Duncan, each grabbing an elbow, glared down at him.

"Oops!" exclaimed Brian. "Oops?"

The voices grew nearer.

"I could have been killed!"

"You dented my motor!"

Bob came into sight as he rounded the corner of the drive, half leading, half dragging a more than dishevelled member of the paparazzi.

"This," Bob exclaimed on seeing them, "says he's been

shot at. Anyone care to explain?"

"The gardener must have set off some bird scarers. Verminous creatures ruin the bark and crap on everything," Sir Arthur replied.

"Ah." Bob looked from one to the other and wiped his hands on the knees of his trousers.

"So it wasn't actually a firearm of any sort?"

They all three shook their heads.

"Right, well nothing I can do then. If Marco, Harpo and Groucho here say it was bird-scaring. Not much the police can do, eh? Can't help it, after all, how were they to know you'd be up somebody else's tree. Don't suppose you had permission?" Bob asked, failing to keep the happy malice out of his voice. The reporter began to look a little less sure of his position.

"Well not exactly permission," he mumbled.

"Not exactly permission. I see." Bob looked up at the tree and thoughtfully stroked his chin. "You're not local, are you lad?"

"No." The reporter nervously replied; he'd heard tales about what they did to you on the Island and he was beginning to think that they were just possibly not the complete wind-up he had at first imagined.

"Because if you were you'd know that we take rather a strong line on privacy over here. You may be able to get away with sneaking around someone's garden and hiding in their shrubbery across but here – well it's almost a capital offence."

The reporter looked from one to the other, and seeing that he was clearly not going to receive any support or indeed sympathy, attempted to stand. Shakily, he picked himself up.

"Don't suppose you have a phone I could use?" he asked rather hopelessly, brushing bits of leaf mould and bark from the folds of his jumper. Before Sir Arthur could think of anything sufficiently sarcastic, Bob intervened, a smile of almost benign sweetness on his face.

"Duncan here will give you a lift to the hospital," he stated kindly, laying a heavy hand on the journalist's shoulder.

"What? Oh no, it's all right I can get a taxi …"

"No, no I insist. Better get yourself checked over."

Brian and Duncan exchanged surprised glances and wondered why Bob was impersonating the Good Samaritan. Carefully taking their cue from Bob they began brushing leaves from the now cringing reporter and as Duncan helpfully pushed him towards his police car, Bob added seriously,

"And you'd better make sure he has one of them tetanus jabs. Nasty place, the countryside, you never know what you might pick up." There was a long silence.

"No, no, I'm fine, really I am. I just need a cup of coffee and a hot bath, that's all," the reporter stuttered as Duncan began to help him into the passenger seat.

"No, no, can't have you being ill on the plane." Bob smiled, showing all his teeth.

"Plane?" asked the reporter, a nervous tic beginning to manifest itself at the side of one eyebrow.

"Yes lad, the one you're going to catch after you've had your jab, packed your things and paid your hotel bill. Or I might start seeing the odd piece of paperwork entitled 'trespass, criminal damage', as that –" Bob turned and pointed at the tall beech, gently swaying in a light breeze, "poor tree will never be the same again, to say nothing of being abusive to a police officer," he added as an afterthought, his face darkening as he remembered one particularly anatomical insult.

Defeated, the journalist slunk into the seat of Duncan's car, still clutching his ruined camera and what looked like the mangled remains of a small mobile phone.

Duncan closed the door for him and grinning broadly, drove off.

Bob thrust his hands deep in the side pockets of his trousers and whistling loudly a snatch of 'A Policeman's Lot is not a Happy One', walked towards the front door.

It was some ten minutes later that they sat in companionable silence sipping coffee in Sir Arthur's study.

"So Detective Inspector, what can I do for you?"

"You can have a look at these documents – carefully mind and with gloves on – which I have a pair of somewhere. And then I'm going to ask you two questions."

"Which are?"

"What, if anything, do you know about the death of your son-in-law, Charles Cholmondley, and have you ever heard of a Professor Bergman?"

"Oh." Sir Arthur glanced at them both over the rim of his coffee cup, a thoughtfully blank expression on his face, and carefully pulling on the plastic gloves, inspected the papers that Tavistock had held little more than an hour earlier.

After reading the scraps of parchment he sighed and gently handing them back to Bob, slowly removed the gloves.

"I see." He took a deep breath before continuing. "Where did you get these?"

"From someone who may or may not be involved with one or possibly two murders."

Sir Arthur's hands shook slightly, the paper emitting faint rustles as if a large snake were slithering over short dry grass. Steeling himself for the kind of verbal chess he hadn't had to play since his retirement, he continued cautiously. "I'm not sure whether anything I can tell you could possibly be of any help but I will tell you all I know," Sir Arthur promised with a crocodile smile, as he carefully set down his cup and steepled his fingers. Bob's years of experience began sending out frantic 'take care' messages down his spine, as he settled himself further back in his seat.

"The letter signed by Professor Bergman was to me. I wondered why it went missing and now I know. My son-in-law was a thief. My daughter suspected but I paid him off before he could do any real damage to her or to the family name. He was both a weak man and a greedy one, not a good combination if you want to keep on the right side of the law." Bob nodded as Sir Arthur, eyes glinting, carried on. "Charles would find rare works and then help to smuggle them out of whichever country he happened to be plundering at the time. I believe my grandson did something similar whilst at university." There was a slight pause as Sir Arthur wiped a dribble of saliva from his mouth. "As for that other matter you wanted to know about, it is quite simply that Professor Bergman was interned here during the war. We met and became friends. He and his wife were cultured intelligent people who had fled from Germany in the early thirties."

"Why did he come here?"

"I told you," Sir Arthur replied shortly.

"No, I don't think so," Bob remarked, his eyes narrowed and his ears craning for the little nuggets of truth he might find.

Sir Arthur, viewing his new adversary with a good deal of respect, paused, revising his next speech. He would, he thought, have to be a little more careful. "He was very interested in the history of the island. He excavated and catalogued some of the major sites of historic importance. With I might add, the blessing of the Manx government. Some of the locals helped and many of the internees."

"And was he searching for anything specific?" Bob asked.

"Well ..."

"The Grail for instance?" Bob stated, all innocence. Sir Arthur paled and paused before answering.

"That was just a fanciful story, Inspector."

"That St Patrick visited the island and left the Grail here?"

"Yes. But it has no basis in fact. At best a scribbled message on old slate buried under the earth by monks who were not even alive at the time. At worst a collective memory handed down from one generation to the other being freely embellished as the centuries went by."

"So you don't think that the Grail is hidden here?"

"No," Sir Arthur lied.

Bob continued as if he'd heard no reply. "If it was, just exactly how much of a motive would it be for murder?"

"You mean how much would it be worth?"

Bob nodded. Brian, who had followed the conversation in silence with a look of incredulity plastered over his face waited with bated breath for the answer.

"Well I'm no expert but if it was wooden ... I'd say it would have disintegrated by now. If it was metal and protected in some way then it could be priceless. Even if it was a cup used by St Patrick and could be substantiated by some form of recognised contemporary evidence then I'd say that in principle you would be able to name your own price."

"Which was why your son-in-law went off into the desert?" Sir Arthur gave up and giving a little sign of surrender with his hands began to answer Bob's questions with a good deal more honesty. Bob, noting the change in body language, visibly relaxed.

"Possibly, if he found evidence left by the early Christian Jews or gentiles. It could have happened. I always thought he had got too greedy and had fallen out with his partners in crime. The body was never found, so who knows?"

"Who indeed," Bob agreed.

"There was one thing about Bergman's visit that you should know."

"Yes?"

"I was over here to sniff out an agent."

"The Tidemaster, you told us that the last time we spoke," Bob remarked, his eyes narrowing.

"Yes. Sources in Germany advised us that he was sent here under the express instructions of Herr Hitler."

"Why?"

"The Grail."

"What?"

"Hitler had this idea that holy relics would help him in his fight. He would have divine aid. He collected them from across the globe and if he'd got his hands on something believed to be the cup used by Christ during the Last Supper, the propaganda alone could have changed the course of history."

"In what way?" Brian asked, interested.

"Well, for instance, let's just say that if Hitler had had it in his possession when he had us on the run before Dunkirk he might have just kept going and actually invaded us."

Brian looked horrified as the implied future hit him.

"We weren't ready, everyone knew that. We played for time and got it but without that pause we might have lost. I'm not saying we would have but we might."

"Because of some old cup?" Brian exclaimed.

"Yes, because of some old cup," Bob agreed thoughtfully.

They sat in silence for a while.

Bob stood up and walked to the window.

"Do you know if the good professor found anything?"

"I think he discovered where it might have been taken but he couldn't get to it. He told everyone that the cup had remained in Ireland. That he had new evidence to prove it and then he concentrated on the remaining digs for the rest of the war.

"I was by then caught up in the riots in Douglas, which I believe have already been well documented. The man I knew as the Tidemaster was one of the alleged victims but I have my doubts."

"Doubts?"

"The riot coincided within a week with the professor discontinuing his search. I believe that my quarry, scenting defeat, left the Island the night of the riot and made his way over to Ireland."

"So who was the riot victim?"

"I don't know. But I do know that a burnt body leaves very little evidence. We had no laboratories, no DNA tests, no modern forensic help."

"Easily done then."

"Very easy and something which he'd done before, in Europe and in England."

"Anything else?"

"No."

"How did he get here?"

"Well, he was reputed to be a fascist. I think he came over with a group of well to do, woolly-minded, nazi sympathisers." The scorn in Sir Arthur's voice was still palpable even after a gap of over fifty years.

"He was a political prisoner then?" Brian asked.

"On the face of it, yes. But in reality I still believe he was one of Hitler's elite."

"So what you are saying is that someone could have found all the old references to the Grail and is hunting it down, killing anyone that gets too close?" Brian remarked, frowning.

"Or ..." Bob mused. "They may already know where it is and they are desperately trying to stop any one else finding it."

"That is, of course, another way of looking at it." Sir Arthur gave him a sharp look.

Bob, looking him straight in the eye, wondered if Sir Arthur had indeed told him everything. He had a hunch that something, some small piece of evidence was being held back by Sir Arthur, but short of the judicial application of thumbscrews, or some form of truth serum it would be impossible to prise out.

"Right well, I guess that's it then. We go and see our suspect and let him know we think we know what he's after."

"I wish you luck with your search, Inspector. There is one other thing ..."

"Yes?"

"I would appreciate this being kept off the record ..."

"I can't guarantee anything but as long as it doesn't directly involve my investigation and ultimate prosecution," Bob tentatively agreed.

"I suppose you can't say fairer than that. My grandson is not the most attractive of human beings; in fact he takes after his father in rather too many ways. He is also on the warpath and thinks that the ancient muck raked up by those documents will hurt his political career in some way. To be perfectly honest I doubt that even his rogue of a father would have stooped to some of the things he has. His penchant for very young girls for instance ..."

Bob and Brian exchanged telling glances.

"... But he does have friends in high places so take this as a warning. Don't expect him to tell the truth about anything if he thinks he can get away with a lie – and watch your backs."

"You don't like him much do you?"

"I don't like him at all!"

Later, as they drove back to Douglas, Bob wondered just what exactly it was that the honourable member had done that had upset his grandfather so badly. Or perhaps it was very simple; they just couldn't stand each other.

***

Brian collapsed onto the sofa with a heartfelt sigh of relief. Caroline handed him a large glass of ice-cold lager and sat down beside him, curling her feet under her.

"You look," he observed lovingly, "like an elf."

"Do I?" she replied in a pleased voice.

"Yes. The sort of pretty looking thing that would swap babies and hide cows in rocks." Brian added. "Whatever it is, I'm not doing it. I'm going to have something to eat and then I'm going to sleep for more than two hours."

Caroline watched him warily and then stroked the back of his neck with long, slender fingers.

"It's all ready, I did us a pasta bake and some salad," she cooed soothingly.

Brian looked up; nothing, he knew, was this good.

"What are you up to?" he demanded.

"You, my love, have a nasty suspicious mind," she retorted, getting up and moving towards the corner that their landlord euphemistically called a kitchen.

"I've been thinking about the wedding, and I was wondering about maybe having it earlier, rather than later," she called out, as she bent to remove the Pyrex dish from the oven.

Brian sniffed the air, now redolent with the smell of garlic, herbs, tomatoes and onions and sighed appreciatively.

"I thought you wanted to have a year to plan it properly?" he said, getting up and walking to their small dining table, already set with cutlery, flowers, glasses and a bottle of opened Chianti. "That's why you and your mother have been pouring over those glossy magazines, and we need a mortgage before we even get to see a house," he said, as she deposited the dish on a large cork mat and he carefully poured out two glasses of wine.

"Well, I thought maybe we could have a small, simple church wedding with a light lunch afterwards and a week in Scotland. We could take the car and drive round, it would be fun and you could go fishing," she added, watching him carefully for signs of surrender.

"Fishing?" Brian asked, taking the bait.

"Yes love, after all I think those magazines deliberately put up the cost to keep the advertisers happy. Mum reckons we could do the whole thing for about six thousand."

"Six thousand!" Brian nearly choked on his wine.

"Yes," Caroline agreed, helping herself to the salad.

"But we don't have a spare thousand at the moment, let alone six."

"Ah," Caroline smiled at him, taking an envelope from the folds of her skirt and passing it over the table to him.

"What's this?" Brian asked.

"Read it," Caroline replied.

Brian unfolded the envelope and extracted a thin rectangle of paper from it. He had to look at it twice for it to sink in. "Bloody hell, it's a cheque."

"Yes."

"A cheque for twenty thousand Australian dollars!"

"Father sent it, it came this morning."

"Your father! But I thought …" His voice trailed off, puzzled.

"I rang him a couple of days ago and well, we said a lot of things maybe we should have said before and as you have kindly pointed out on numerous occasions, I have to grow up sometime. Besides Mother made me," she added as an afterthought.

"Oh. Just exactly how much is this?" Brian asked, fingering the cheque nervously.

"I'm not sure but whatever it is, your father says he will

match it."

Brian stared at her open mouthed.

"It's not all for the wedding, it's for a deposit on a house," Caroline advised. "That's why Mum and I thought we'd pare things down a bit, do it cheaper, that way we can have enough left over for something new, low-maintenance, with a bit of garden space, and two or maybe three bedrooms?"

"A real home." Brian stared around him, taking in the cheap paper, threadbare carpet and the peeling paint for almost the first time.

He sat silently regarding his plate before pushing it to one side.

"What is the matter?" Caroline asked. "I thought you'd be over the moon, not looking as if I'd tried to forcefeed you strychnine!"

"I'm so bloody lucky, it scares me," he replied, moving towards her.

"Why?" she asked, looking up at him. This was not going the way she had very carefully planned, she thought to herself.

"Hold me," he muttered. Caroline stood and wrapped her arms around him.

"What's brought this on?" she asked, her voice barely a whisper.

"Chelsea Thomas. Her fiancé told me they were going to get married because she was pregnant. Only?"

"What?" Caroline gently prompted.

"She wasn't. Or at least not according to the pathologist, she wasn't. Caroline, I couldn't tell him, nobody could. It was truly awful. You know I was watching him and thinking of us." His voice trailed away.

"Us?"

"The difference; if something happened to you, I'd die. That poor chap was upset not because he'd lost Chelsea but because of a baby that didn't even exist. I know you shouldn't speak ill of the dead, but if anyone had to go they couldn't have chosen a more unpopular victim than young Chelsea. Even her parents seemed relieved. Do you know she'd managed to scrounge thousands off them because of her condition?" Brian sighed and kissed the side of Caroline's neck.

Caroline looked up at him, an oddly thwarted expression in her eyes.

"So what is it that you think requires wine, cold pasta and warm salad to tell me?" he asked.

"Nothing, just wanted to surprise you with the cheque, that's all," she lied, turning before he could see the frustration in her eyes. "You sit back down while I put the pasta back in the microwave to warm up."

Chapter 9

Ian Felton-Cholmondley ground his teeth and inhaled sharply. This was going to be difficult, very difficult. But that idiot Lawrence had got him into this and he had no intention of sinking any deeper. It had been containable when only the press had been involved but now the police were snooping around. It wasn't as if he could call in any favours over a quiet word over a round of golf or lunch at the club. This was the Isle of Man and he had absolutely no illusions as to his popularity there.

The telephone rang insistently. Reluctantly he picked it up and listened.

"No, I have nothing to say."

There was a pause followed by a flood of muttered sound alternating in volume as the speaker, running out of steam, stopped.

"Listen you bitch! I have nothing, absolutely nothing, to say on this subject or any other." Furiously he slammed the phone back down and then savagely ripped the wire out of the telephone socket.

"Intolerable, intolerable," he muttered over and over again. He thought briefly of summoning some sort of aid from his Party until he realised they would be more than delighted to be rid of him. He'd been warned last time not to expect any help from that particular corner. Some on the Island were already saying that he was doing nothing for his native land. Native land: a rock squatting in the Irish Sea, cold, damp and inescapable. For heaven's sake it was missing from more maps than it was on! Even the fabled landmass of Atlantis had featured more often in the works of cartographers. Perhaps there was one person he could call. The Minister – it was election year after all and he was the last person to want a scandal. 'And if it all went wrong?' Ian gave himself a mental shake. 'Who the hell cared anyway?'

Extracting his mobile he carefully ran down the index and finding what he wanted, punched in two digits.

"It's me ... No, you listen; I still have the pictures ... I know what I promised at the time but even negatives can be copied ... Exactly! I believe the new kid on the block is already snapping at your heels, so perhaps I ought to send them to him. Or possibly that rather nice lady you married? I don't have time to go into that. So listen. I want you to call off the hounds, in particular some nosey parker of a policeman called Bob Callow. No I don't know his rank ... Does it matter what he says I've done? Speak to the Chief Constable and get him sent on some course. Isn't that what you normally do? I need time – a day or two at most to tidy things up ... I haven't done anything except speak to people who are no longer with us. Unfortunately my ex-wife seems to think this could be payback time and is digging up the sort of muck that most journalists can only dream of. If you throw me to the wolves I shall ensure that you end up on the menu too ... Two days and you won't hear from me again."

Slowly he disconnected and moved towards the window. Down below people scurried to or from whichever meeting their respective assistants and secretaries had arranged. Black taxis, horns blaring, ducked and dived between the slowly moving vehicles. The tall, ornately carved buildings stood like sentinels on either side of a black shimmering tarmac river. Ian opened the windows a little more to catch an elusive breath of air, untainted by smells of diesel, hot humanity and the River Thames.

He wiped his forehead with a crisply laundered handkerchief and closed his eyes, leaning his whole body against the wooden frame.

He needed to focus, to stay calm and concentrate. First he must pack a few things and order a plane and then a boat. He only needed a single ticket. If only that fool Lawrence hadn't blown it. No matter, he knew where to look and that was the important thing, not the destiny of some washed-up writer with a drink problem and an overworked imagination.

***

The Chief Constable paced his office with the barely concealed ferocity of a Bengal tiger with toothache. He seethed and ranted internally.

Bob entered the room just as he'd turned and they met almost head on.

"Sit down Bob. Coffee?" Charm, never far from the surface, took over the well-oiled cogs, the machinery moving back into leader mode.

"Er yes." Bob nervously eyed his boss. The glittering eyes and heightened colour were a dead giveaway. After years of avoiding any form of unpleasantness, normally domestic, with the call of "I'll go and get a paper then?" he could now spot the signs of a major eruption at twenty paces. He just prayed it was nothing to do with him. Although, he thought with gathering hopefulness, that as he had after all been offered a cup of the Boss's most excellent brew, it probably wasn't.

Depositing a mug of aromatic liquid, dark as creosote and about as strong, in front of his subordinate the Chief Constable lowered himself into his own chair and glared at the phone. He could almost see the smoke from his previous conversation with the minister gently curling into the air.

"I hear you have been upsetting our illustrious Member for Europe?" he asked, watching Bob for any telltale signs of lying.

"News travels fast I see," Bob replied, calmly meeting his gaze.

"I've just had the minister on the phone begging for clemency."

"Ah," Bob muttered, the dawn of understanding descending on him from a great height.

"That must have been fun," he added.

"That man had the temerity to ask me to ask you, to lay off! Lay off! First he wants a result then when we look like we might have one he tells me, no – orders me, to forget it! I will not be told what to do by someone more interested in his own political skin than in justice and the safety of everyone on this Island!"

Bob sat slightly stunned.

There was a silence while the last pumice stones fell to earth together with a variety of poisoned ash. Nothing more was said so Bob assumed that Vesuvius had closed down for the foreseeable future.

"I gather he wasn't happy about our investigations." Bob thought about adding a 'sir' but didn't want to be seen to creep.

"You could say that." The Chief Constable scowled and took a measured gulp of coffee; the scowl deepened.

"He said we ought to be concentrating on the film crew and not on this Island's indispensable, internationally renowned … argh … makes me ill to think about it."

"Doesn't sound like anyone I'm investigating, to be honest, sir. As far as I can gather our beloved Euro MP is according to various sources a lying, cheating, weak, greedy dishonest son of a lying, cheating, dishonest small-time crook. No one has as yet mentioned the word blackmail but he fits the standard profile."

"Wonder what he has on our beloved leader?" the Chief Constable mused, his voice warming slightly.

"Exactly my thoughts – and knowing a little more about the sod I'd say it was of an unpleasantly carnal nature and involved being manacled to a bed, wearing a nappy and being beaten with damp vegetable matter."

"Really?" The office temperature began to rise, as the Chief Constable thought happy thoughts.

"No, but one can dream. I expect it's something more mundane like making a whole batch of promises and then reneging and I bet it's on paper. Probably not half as bad as the minister thinks, with a totally logical explanation."

"Oh." The Chief Constable felt slightly disappointed; he'd hoped for at least some sort of sex scandal, however unlikely. Visibly calming, he fished around in the drawer at the side of his desk and extracted a small tin of the sugar-dusted shortbread of which he was inordinately fond.

Carefully he handed one to Bob, laid one on a piece of memo paper and replaced the tin.

"On the other hand, our Euro hero does appear to have been a very naughty boy and I have no reason to believe that this particular leopard has any intention of changing his spots."

"Good."

"I wonder?"

"What?"

"Just exactly what it is that I'm so close to, that Ian Felton-Cholmondley feels he has no other option but to try to call me off."

"You have no idea, not even half an idea?"

"Well ..." Bob hesitated.

"Go on."

"I think somebody is trying to find something he or she thinks was hidden on the island over a thousand years ago. If they did find something, however small a scrap and it could be authenticated, some buyer somewhere would pay the earth to have it."

"And just what is it that would be worth that much?"

"The Grail."

"What!" The Chief Constable exclaimed, almost choking on his shortbread.

"The cup that ..."

"I know what the Grail is. And you think it came here? Bob – honestly?"

"Well somebody does, and they believe it enough to kill. One chap who we know was investigating the possibility was drowned and a young reporter was raped and then murdered because she was asking questions about the same thing. I also have letters and papers relating to an old search conducted by an eminent Professor of Archaeology who was over here during the Second World War. Even Hitler was convinced enough to send one of his top men over."

"Ah – shades of the Lost Ark."

"Exactly."

"The whole thing sounds highly suspect." There was a slight pause as the information was cerebrally digested. "Speaking of which, how is our prime suspect?"

"We may have to let him go."

"Go? Why?"

"Well he fits the frame very well. He knew both victims. He was seen walking down to the beach with the girl shortly before the attack. He was interested in the Grail story and we think he's very well acquainted with our favourite politician but …"

"I gather I'm not going to like this."

"No and to be honest I've sent more blood off for testing. The DNA found in the semen from the last victim was almost exactly the same as that of Samuel Lawrence with one exception. It apparently carried one particular genetic characteristic."

"I really am not going to like this, am I?"

"No. And nor to be entirely truthful, do I. Our murderer is an albino."

"Ah."

"Everything else checks out. But as Mr Lawrence is patently not an albino we will have to let him go if the second batch of results is the same. Except that I know he did it or he was with the killer and therefore knows who did do it!"

"What does Lawrence say?"

"Sticks to the same story: he was finding information for someone. He met both victims but that they left him safe and well, if not entirely sober. That he had a drink and fell asleep after the girl had gone and he can't remember anything else. He has no alibi and we have witnesses who think they saw him in the right place at the right time."

"But no solid evidence,"

"No."

"Right, well if the results are negative, let him go. But I want him watched. Put him on 24-hour surveillance. If it isn't him he's close to whoever it is."

"Good, saves me asking."

"Right. And Bob?"

"Yes."

"This time try to bring me a live and visible murderer. To lose one might be considered unfortunate but to lose two …"

"Looks like sheer carelessness!" Bob riposted with a

grin and then, remembering the outcome of the previous year's murder enquiry, shuddered. Bob could still, when he remembered, almost taste the warm iron tang of blood on his face.

The Chief Constable, also remembering, deliberately broke the spell by almost banging his china mug back down on the polished wood surface of his desk.

"Well that appears to be it. Remember I want this one wrapped up as soon as possible and I don't want any more bodies found dripping on any more beaches. Understood?"

"Yes sir."

"Good, keep me informed. And get someone to sit on the press. I do not want to read about your antics in the local rag before I've been briefed by you in this very room."

Bob sighed heavily and stood up. The audience was over. With any luck by the time he got back to his desk the new test results would be in and he could make an arrest. He just had an uncomfortable feeling that luck was something that he was running out of fast.

***

Samuel Lawrence sat hunched over the plastic chair he was seated upon and closed his eyes. Questions, questions and yet more questions. He was very tired, tired and confused. He couldn't see what else he could say that he hadn't said already, at least twice. He heard the door open and the sound of a chair being scraped across the floor. Opening his eyes he saw the by now familiar form of Detective Inspector Callow. He groaned, his body sagging deeper into the hard plastic outline of his chair.

"That's not very nice. Most people are usually pleased to see me." Bob grinned, pushing over a mug of tea. "Milk and two sugars wasn't it?"

"Yes thanks," Samuel muttered, hugging the mug to him and staring into its steamy depths.

"So we've gone through everything at least twice but for the sake of Duncan here let's just go through it one more time."

"What have I got to lose but my liberty?" Samuel wrily joked, but no one laughed and there was a brief stony silence. Duncan fiddled with the tape machine and spoke the words required by law when interviewing a suspect. Samuel Lawrence stared at the wall; he'd heard it all before but he had no intention of letting them see how much it still affected him now.

Bob cleared his throat and in the sepulchral tones he always reserved for interviews with his main suspect, began. "You say in your previous statement, that on the evening that Barney Goldsmith met a watery end you were in your holiday flat reading. There were no witnesses and you didn't go out at all from the moment you returned from a meal at the Mona Lisa at 8.30 p.m. to the following morning?"

"Yes."

"And you have no idea who could have lured him down to the beach, despite the fact that according to our phone records you rang his hotel number and spent twenty-three minutes talking to someone in room forty-six. Which, in case you are wondering, was Mr Goldsmith's room. The girl on reception said Mr Goldsmith left the hotel ten minutes after your call finished, she remembers because he said he would miss dinner and she gave him a small bar of chocolate to tide him over."

"Coincidence," Samuel muttered morosely.

"A sheep's head arrives in a suitcase from a London flight, together with a note to Sir Arthur Felton referring to the Tidemaster. Odd name, that, don't you think? But then maybe not; after all it was you that asked for certain government documents to be released and I believe they referred to the same odd name."

"He was an agent during the war. I came across his name when I was researching a programme for Channel Four." Samuel took a long sip of tea, refusing to meet Bob's gimlet-sharp eyes.

"So the fact that a threat was enclosed with the head of a sheep was another coincidence. Nothing to do with someone being given the idea from another script you wrote for Carlton Television. A script, I might add, which was never used and very few people actually saw."

"I can explain ..."

"I was rather hoping you might."

"I gave the idea to Barney. He said he wanted to play a practical joke on an ex-lover. I didn't ask who the ex was. I told him about the head. I don't know why, sheer devilment perhaps. I honestly didn't think it would get through customs. It was a play on words, a threat like in the Godfather. A friend of his who has a farm agreed to get hold of the head and freeze it. Another friend of Barney's stuck it on the plane.

"Barney said he'd left stuff behind in his flat. They checked onto the plane with their and Barney's case. It was just a joke and before you ask I have no idea who it was."

"We do – a cretin called Adam Pictown. He admitted it to the local police when they went round to Barney's flat."

"Oh."

"So who was Barney trying to blackmail?"

"He held a grudge against Ian Felton-Cholmondley. Ian raped his sister, or at least Barney believed it was rape, as the girl was under the influence of drugs and alcohol. Mr Political said she'd agreed, they had a date, he took her out to dinner then one thing led to another. It was by all accounts pretty brutal but the girl refused to press charges and Mr Charm agreed to pay for the abortion."

"Good God!"

"Nice man, don't you think? A real role model! Barney said he wanted to upset the family although by all accounts they seem to hate him more than anyone else, particularly his grandfather."

"And that's all he wanted to talk to you about?" Bob asked, his voice dripping with distrust.

Even Duncan noted the slight hesitation before Samuel replied. "No, nothing else."

"You also met and talked to Chelsea Thomas, a local reporter?" Bob continued, rocking back in his chair and staring at the ceiling.

"Yes. Look we have already been through all of this."

"But I think something is missing, so we will go through it again."

"If we must."

"Oh I really think we must." Bob crossed his arms, his face implacable.

"Chelsea called me. She said she'd spoken to some chap in London who had seen me talking to young Barney. She said that I could talk to her or the police. Well, I chose her. I wish I'd just gone to you lot myself but frankly I had no alibi the night Barney died and I thought I could reason with her."

"And did you reason with her?" Bob enquired, carefully inspecting his fingernails.

"Yes. We had a chat. I told her about the research Barney had been doing and I let slip a few things about Ian Felton-Cholmondley's past and that of his father. I didn't honestly think it would do any harm. We had a drink together, a glass or two of red wine. I walked her to the door and that was the last time I saw her," Samuel declared, his voice suddenly shrill.

"I have a statement here in front of me, signed by a reliable source, in fact from, before you start with the doubting Thomas bit, one of our nosiest neighbourhood watchers. Who says quite categorically that she saw you and Miss Thomas laughing and giggling as you walked down the road together. She also said that you had your arms around her and that she reckoned you were off to the beach for 'a bit of R&R' is the expression she used."

"Chance would be a fine thing," Samuel retorted.

"Pardon?"

"I'm impotent, have been for years. Frankly my dear I couldn't get it up even if I had the full chorus of Chippendales and two litres of aromatic massage oil! I doubt whether anything would work. And I did not leave the house that night. Did the old bag actually see my face? Did she?" he screamed, standing up and pushing the chair away from him. Duncan made a slight movement towards him but Bob shook his head and muttered, "Leave him," under his breath.

"She says it was you."

"But did she see my face?" Samuel shouted.

"Would you like me to ask her?" Bob enquired sweetly.

"No. I will."

"Sit down!" Bob growled.

Samuel stood against the wall, arms folded.

"I said sit down," Bob repeated. Samuel, hearing the edge to Bob's voice, walked back to his chair and with a display of sulkiness that would have impressed a four-year-old, sat. They remained silently glaring at each other, eyes locked. Duncan coughed nervously.

"Duncan."

"Yes sir?"

"Give this lady a ring and see if she's able to get down and have a look at our man here. You can toddle off and give her a lift if she wants one. Because frankly the sooner we sort this out the better." Bob handed a slip of paper to Duncan who gave it a brief look and tucked it into his pocket.

"Anyone can dress like me and anyone else can think that the dress is me."

"Point taken. Right, well, that seems to be that. Oh there was just one more thing."

"What?"

Bob stood up, carefully unbending weary limbs.

"Just exactly who are you trying to find the Grail for? I mean, I presume this person has a buyer already and I also presume he or she is paying you well for his or her services?"

Samuel Lawrence ran his tongue around lips suddenly dry and tried to conjure up a brief smile.

"I'm sure I don't know what you mean."

"No. I rather think you do. Only I'd like you to work out whether this someone is paying you enough."

"I'm sorry?"

"The death penalty may have been outlawed over here but if you are found guilty of not one but two murders, I'd say you are looking at a very long time in the Jurby Hilton. At your age, life would certainly mean life. Because if you aren't our murderer somebody somewhere is very keen for us to think you are."

"But the DNA test?"

"Almost a perfect match."

"What!"

Bob smiled his alligator smile and muttered a few brief words for the benefit of the tape. Duncan fiddled with the machine and quietly left the room accompanied by Bob, his final parting shot still hanging in the air.

Samuel Lawrence, suddenly alone, sank back into the hard plastic contours of his chair, rested his head on his hands and wept.

Chapter 10

Tavistock and Gloria waded through dark blue, green-streaked water to reach the rock on which Chelsea had fought her last fight.

Together they hauled themselves onto the warm sun-drenched slab and sat panting in the hot noon haze. Gloria, looking around, shuddered and despite the warmth, hugged her long cotton shirt tighter.

"So this is it!" she exclaimed.

"Apparently so," Tavistock agreed, kneeling down and peering into the murky weed-tangled depths on the seaward side of their rocky island.

"Gives me the willies," Gloria muttered, moving so that she could lie on her stomach next to her friend.

"How long have we known each other?" she asked, gently trailing her hand in the light-dappled water.

"Since you were a mere blot," Tavistock replied.

"So you know that I don't often imagine things? And despite my job I'm not naturally vindictive."

"What about that story on Susan Nordley?" Tavistock asked, raising an expressive eyebrow.

Gloria giggled. "She was an idiot. Besides book sales went up not down so she should have been grateful."

"She had to move and someone threw petrol through

her letterbox. I'm not sure she'd be overjoyed to see you," Tavistock replied before adding through wrily-pursed lips. "And frankly if you'd done it to me I would have lurked outside your office with a couple of friendly bouncers and broken all your appendages – and I like you!"

"I didn't know that the petrol thing would happen," Gloria muttered almost shamefacedly.

"Cause and effect love, cause and effect." Tavistock sat back on her heels and surveyed the scene of the crime.

"I still don't see how anyone could possibly get here if not willingly and under their own steam. And why didn't she cry out? There are houses up there. It wasn't late. There are still people walking dogs, couples of either sex grabbing kisses, leaving the local, so why didn't she scream? I would have."

"Perhaps because she either liked it or she thought there was a story in it?" Gloria mused.

"A story?"

"Look, if Chelsea thought it was just rough sex and then she could write some scandalous exposé she'd have agreed to almost anything. I saw the place she was living in. God, I remember what it's like. All your money goes on clothes, a motor, socialising. You have to impress and her place was a dump. Really grim, to live there would have made her hungry as hell."

"So whom did she socialise with?"

"No one from the paper unless they could help it. Particularly the lads, they hated her more than I did."

"Surely not."

"Oh you'd be surprised at how unpopular she was. For starters she'd drop her knickers for anyone. The janitor upwards, if she thought it would either give her a promotion or a story. She lied as if the truth meant nothing at all. That girl had absolutely no integrity or ethical awareness in any shape or form and she stole."

"Stole?"

"Stories. You could work on something, leave it to have a cuppa or go out to lunch, come back and there it would be on page three with her name underneath. She didn't do it to me, not unless you count taking that phonecall and getting herself killed, but she did it to at least three of her contemporaries. Actually she was up for review and there was talk of asking her to leave on the grounds that she was causing an atmosphere."

"What about her fiancé? He must have loved her surely!"

"Well I only met him the once, before Christmas, but I'd lay money on the fact that he's not too distressed."

"How the hell do you work that one out?" Tavistock exclaimed, shocked.

"Because he gave me the impression of a hunted rabbit that's why."

"Oh."

"If you ask me she forced him into the engagement; his parents are loaded."

"But you still feel guilty?"

"Yes. I couldn't stand her and yet I feel as if I should do something to catch the man that did this. We all do."

"This place must have been very uncomfortable," Tavistock mused.

"I really can't see Samuel Lawrence luring her here though."

"Why?"

"She would have been wary. Old man, lonely beach. Besides she liked her men just a few years older than herself. I just can't see it," Gloria muttered, closing her eyes.

Tavistock sat back and leant against the curve of black slate.

They sat in silence as the water ebbed and flowed, lulling them both towards the world of waking dreams.

"Nice ... Very nice ... Soft and pleasurable ... Golden cream ... Want to let me smooth those curves and bury my hardness in your soft warm wetness? My pretty, pretty."

"What?" Tavistock sat up, suddenly wide awake and stared around her. Gloria mumbled in her sleep, lulled by the movement of water and the heat of the sun.

"Lower, lower ... That's it ... Look into the deep pool of my eyes ... Look deep into ..."

"No!" Tavistock screamed. Gloria, her hand slipping into the cool water was startled to find herself being half pulled, half shoved back from the water's edge.

"What the hell's the matter with you?"

"Didn't you see, couldn't you hear?"

"What?"

"You didn't see or hear anything?" Tavistock asked incredulously.

"No. I was nearly asleep, having a nice dream if you must know. Quite sexy too."

Tavistock moved a strand of hair from her eyes and waited for her pulse rate to slow down. Gloria watched her, a worried frown on her face.

"What sort of dream?" Tavistock asked.

"Sort of being made love to kind of dream."

"What did he look like?"

"Oh I don't know. A long-haired Robbie Williams, Hugh Grant. I wasn't actually concentrating on his face. Lovely voice though."

"Voice?"

"Sexy, masculine, you know. Good God Tavistock, you're a writer, you work it out!" Gloria laughed.

"Come on."

"Where?"

"Anywhere but here."

Gloria, bemused, watched her friend lower herself onto the sand and pebbles furthest away from the ebbing waves. Gloria had never seen her look like this; she looked as though she was scared stiff.

"Will you get off that rock?" Tavistock shouted.

"All right, all right, keep your hair on."

Gloria grudgingly followed Tavistock back to the road that ran alongside the beach.

Tavistock stood at the top of the concrete steps leading from the beach to the pebble-strewn turning place and screwing up her eyes, stared at the stone slab they had just left. There was nothing there and yet she knew they were being watched. A cold chill spread from the tips of her fingers to her stomach. She would have lunch with Gloria as they had planned and then she would find Mannanan, even if she had to scour the Island to do so.

* * *

Mannanan stood amidst the wild grasses and soft ground roses that covered the old fort at Burroo Ned and watched the flash of gulls as they dived towards the Calf of Man and an approaching fishing boat. The boat, jaunty in its coat of sky blue, dipped and jumped through the waves. White foam frothed and curled around it and in its wake, gulls dived into the sparkling water hunting for scraps. Before the tide could turn against it, water boiling between rocks, sharp as giant's teeth, the little boat flung itself between the Island's coast and the Calf. Dodging the cliff and rock on either side, using the channels that only the sea workers knew.

Seals barked a welcome from their stony armchairs and with a shout, a fish was thrown their way. Mannanan smiled. He remembered old Orry Collister always opening a can of pilchards when he came this way. Orry and Maigret the seal. He sighed; he could almost hear that day of storms when Orry rescued the pup, caught in his lines. Injured and with heart racing, the pup had looked at Orry without fear as a defenceless child would its parent. Orry had taken the pup in, named it Maigret after his favourite book, and then when it was well, had released it with a heavy heart, back into the sea. Maigret, never really forgetting his strange, webless father, would wait at the entrance to the churning passage between the rocks and every time he returned, Orry would toss Maigret a few of his catch.

One storm-tossed night, Orry returned from the fishing grounds, but Maigret failed to come. Anxiously, Orry paced the floor of his small cottage and the next morning as the storm abated in glowing glints of grey and gold, he and his friends put to sea and searched. They found the seal battered and bruised two days later and brought him home.

One night, a year almost to the day of the great storm, Orry died. Quietly and with dignity, he went to sleep, watching Liverpool lose, his pipe slipping gently from his mouth and the mug of tea, untouched, congealing slowly at his side.

Maigret waited every night for his return. Mannanan remembered the inconsolable seal, so patient in his grief. He had intervened then, talking to Orry's son in his dreams, reasoning the unreasonable.

That evening young Peter had set out to sea and slowing his father's boat, waited patiently. A head bobbed from the darkening surface and barked. Eyes sparkling, it took the fish and Peter watched it disappear beneath the surface. Tears stinging and mingling with the salt spray tossed towards him by the brightly painted bow, Peter turned the wheel, and engines thumping, headed homewards, the pain of loss shared.

Mannanan smiled into the wind and hugged the pleasure of a deed well done to himself as Peter, now older and still throwing fish to the new pups, sped towards the safety of the harbour wall.

That was where Tavistock found Mannanan, a tall, gaunt figure holding secrets in his head.

"I want to talk to you," she announced, an edge of steel to her voice.

"Oh?" Mannanan, seeing her determined expression took a small step backwards.

"Oh no you don't, matey! In the car."

"What?"

"In the car now, or I shall put you in a book."

"I've been in lots of books," Mannanan smiled, standing his ground.

"Not as some middle-aged warlock who would make Lord Voldemort look like a really nice guy," Tavistock hissed.

"You wouldn't dare!"

"Trust me, I would!"

"So?"

"I can see it now, every paganist, new age guru, dodgy Satanist. They'd all be here dancing naked around the stones up at the Meayl Circle, sacrificing chickens, spilling blood on the ground, fornicating in the open and eating babies!"

"Good God!"

"Now are you going to get in that car? Or do I have to get the laptop out?"

"All right, all right …"

When they were safely seated and Tavistock had ensured there was no one around she picked a slip of paper from the glove compartment and waved it under Mannanan's nose.

"This is a receipt …"

"Does Richard know?" Mannanan sweetly asked.

"Don't get smart with me, buster. You know perfectly

well what this is. Just you wait until Bob finds out. Thought you were being really clever, didn't you!"

"I don't know what you mean."

"That first day at Sir Arthur's. You remember the day I saw that nasty little rape and murder. Bit convenient considering the next but one paper in the pile was this!"

"Ah."

"Remember it now?" Tavistock waved the paper at him again.

"I can explain."

"I bet you can."

"Er …"

"This is a receipt for a boat chartered by Professor Bergman, paid for by Sir Arthur and used by the good professor to have a good look at the coastline around Port Erin and Port St Mary. I don't suppose you could possibly tell me whether he found the entrance to whichever cave you and your little mate St Patrick had hidden the Grail in?"

Mannanan paled and stared at her in stunned amazement.

"How?" His voice tailed off.

"I am not stupid. I found this. Realised there was only one thing the good professor was interested in and put two and two together. I write fiction remember! It wasn't that difficult. And you made me see that … All because I might find this. Why?"

"There is something in the cave with the Grail."

"The Glashton?"

"How?"

"You. You went very odd when I said they were going to film the tale of the Glashton. You tried to hide this and more important than that I heard the evil little bastard try to lure my friend Gloria to a watery and downright horrible death!"

"He can't get out!"

"Ah, so you admit it!" Tavistock shouted triumphantly.

"Look he can't get out because it's all sealed up."

"You sure?"

"Yes."

"Where is this grave?"

"Within the chasms."

"Off we go then." Tavistock started the car and drove at speed out of the car park. Mannanan sat scowling horribly, trying to remember when he'd last checked the cave.

They arrived at the path leading to the chasms and stopped.

"Out you go."

"This is pointless."

"So humour me!"

"Why does Richard stay with you?"

"Because the alternative is his mother and even he's not that stupid."

"Ah."

"Richard, left to his own devices, would starve. Now stop quibbling and get it over with. I shall await your return." Mannanan, observing the set chin and determined gleam in her eyes, which reminded him suddenly of his own mother, gave in and disappeared.

Minutes later he returned.

"We need Bob," he muttered.

"I thought we might," Tavistock muttered grimly. "He's gone hasn't he?"

"Not exactly."

"What does that mean?"

"He's still there but he's stronger and there is a hole."

"Hole?"

"Under the water. There was an entrance from the sea. I sealed it up only someone has unsealed it. And unsealed it very recently."

"The Grail?"

"Still there or at least the spirit is."

"So whoever found the cave –"

"Isn't interested in the Grail."

"Or couldn't see it."

"Maybe," Mannanan admitted grudgingly.

"I'll phone Bob now and arrange a meeting."

Tavistock picked up the mobile, punched numbers and after listening impatiently left a message.

She sat back and drummed her fingers against the plastic-covered steering wheel.

"I heard him, you know. Calling from the water. Felt him too. How can anyone exude that much menace?"

"Because evil, my dear, is ageless. Ageless and very, very, clever."

"Great, I really needed to know that."

Tavistock turned the key in the ignition and rapidly executed a terrifying variation of a three-point turn to the total disbelief of three scared rabbits and a large black crow.

Mannanan, who had closed his eyes, opened them again as they reached the main road.

"This test to be able to drive on the road. You passed it then?"

"Yes?"

"First time?'

"No, Fourth attempt."

"Ah."

"Why?"

"Nothing. Just wondered, that's all."

"Fine. Well while you're wondering you can put a few words together which will explain to Bob just exactly how and why someone or something as old as you is murdering people. Because I for one can't and I have a really big imagination. And by all accounts Bob's boss the Chief

Constable has none at all. So please make it good."

The rest of the journey back to Tavistock's house was continued in silence as Tavistock concentrated on the road and Mannanan dwelt on times past.

***

Bob was just breaking into his own car with a piece of bent wire, when a large hand slapped him on the back and shouted in his ear. "Right then mate, you're nicked!"

Bob, his heart beating wildly, jumped out of several skins and spun backwards.

Greg Matthews, his old friend and ex-partner from training college, stood grinning hugely from the safety of the grass verge.

"Where the bloody hell have you sprung from?" Bob exclaimed, clutching his chest. "You nearly gave me a heart attack."

"On holiday, mate. Same as you should be, according to Moira."

"Ah."

"Well may you say 'Ah', to be honest Bob, old friend, I wouldn't go home for a bit. Moira is spitting nails and I don't just mean the ones that should be in the new decking!"

"What new decking?" Bob asked, going pale.

"Surprised you've got any ears left, would have thought they'd have burnt down to the roots by now." Greg added.

Bob was about to fight back with a few well-chosen words, most of them rude and of a sexual nature when his mobile buzzed frantically in the snug confines of his jacket pocket.

"Oh, bugger it, what now!"

None too pleased he answered it.

"Well … No, I'm not in a bad mood … Why could I possibly be in a foul temper? I've only missed another eagerly anticipated meander through a patch of cumulus … Has she …? What did you say? And she believed that? Streuth! … Where? … Give me forty minutes. I said I would be there didn't I?"

Bob switched the small blue rectangle off and stood silently frowning at it. There were days when he seriously considered tossing it off the nearest bridge!

"Who was that?" Greg asked.

"Tavistock."

"Ah."

"What do you mean, ah?"

"Nothing."

"Look, maybe you didn't see her at her best last year."

"You mean when we were standing six inches above the floor of a house demolished twenty years before whilst watching one of the nastiest murders I could ever imagine?"

"Ah."

"So you going to give me a lift back to your place or not?"

"How do you fancy a little scenic trip?" Bob asked, finally opening the door.

"What sort of trip?" Greg asked suspiciously, climbing into the passenger seat after removing the wad of pilot and do-it-yourself magazines first.

"Does it matter? It's a lovely day the sun is shining, the clouds are white and fluffy and …"

"The tourists are gambolling joyfully upon the hillsides!"

"Something like that."

Bob started the engine and drove off just as Brian erupted from the main doors clutching a piece of closely printed A4 paper. Brian swore loudly and ground his teeth.

There was only one person who might be able to know where Bob was and it wasn't Moira. He just hoped he could remember the number.

***

They met at Chapel Hill, Balladoole. Tavistock, pacing the ground around the stones marking the spot of a Viking ship buried over a thousand years before, turned as they meandered towards her along the tussock-covered pathway. She started at the sight of Greg and smiled broadly.

"Good grief. If I'd known this was a meeting of the three musketeers I'd have brought a hat."

"If I'd known we were meeting up, I'd have brought a copy of Macbeth so I could at least get the words of witch three right!" Greg replied.

Bob looked from one to the other and smiled wickedly, eyes twinkling as he eyed the pair up.

"So why are we here?" Greg asked, sinking down on his haunches to better inspect one of the stones.

"What exactly are these anyway?" he added, feeling the sun-warmed, rough edges. A shiver of something that felt like static electricity stabbed at his fingers.

"This is the site of Professor Bergman's first dig on the Island. The stones mark the outline of a boat in which they believed a Viking chieftain had been interred, together with his weapons, armour and other accoutrements," Tavistock replied, bending down next to him. Mannanan, who had been observing them all from the centre of the boat's remains edged a little closer.

"I'm really not sure this is a good idea," Mannanan muttered, anxiously scanning the area. Bob, watching him, got the distinct impression that he was nervous.

"So what exactly is it that you thought I shouldn't know about?" Bob asked, keeping the anger and frustration he felt under an uneasy check.

"Don't tell me the old guy is back," Greg muttered, looking up.

Mannanan edged backwards as Bob continued to glare at him.

"He is and as he seems to know more than he's been prepared to tell about two rather nasty if not downright horrible deaths, I am at this present moment extremely happy to see him."

Tavistock, Bob and Greg stood around the figure of Mannanan. There was a silence as all three waited for him to speak, standing close enough to each other that the folds of their clothes touched. In the space of a millisecond the ground fell from under their feet and the air darkened. Greg only had time to think, 'Bloody hell – not again!' before they heard the crack of thunder and saw a flash of blue-edged lightning striking the ground beside them.

An elderly gentleman, stocky and bearded, stood up and looked heavenwards. A man standing on the side of the trench he was carefully excavating with a small trowel and what looked like a metal sieve, hunched himself further into his black coat and bent back to his task.

"Professor, do you have any idea how much this would mean to us?" the man in the black coat hissed, removing a stone from the sieve and throwing it back into the pit.

"Will you be careful? That could be valuable," the professor barked, wiping his wet beard with the back of his hand.

"You haven't answered my question," the other man spat, glaring intently at him.

"It isn't here, and if it was by now it would be mere dust. So tell me, an old man, just exactly what your learned and much respected leader would do with it?"

"You may sneer old man, but when we win, with or without your help, I will return and you will pay dearly for your reticence. You and your family."

"Leave my family out of this."

"But I cannot – they are part of you and as such ..." The words hung ominously between them.

The bearded man stood up and took a step towards him, hands clenched into tight fists. "There is nothing here. No cup of Christ, no cave – nothing!"

"Then the slate you found, hidden within this very tomb?"

"A story written by frightened monks a hundred or so years after the event and buried with the man that killed them! And you call that evidence."

"And you don't?"

There was an awkward silence.

"I repeat, there is nothing there."

"Prove it."

"I would if I could."

"Take me to the cave, let me see with my own eyes that there is nothing."

"No."

"No?"

"I dare not."

"Why? Does the creature who guards it frighten you that much?"

"How?"

"Do I know about that particular child of the dammed?"

"Yes."

"I too can read and my master is particularly interested in that little-known tale."

"Why?"

"The Grail would be a relic of immeasurable importance but the creature could be an ally. We could release it back into the world, give it life."

"Do you know what you are suggesting?"

"Oh yes."

"You're mad. Utterly mad."

"Show me the cave!" Quietly he brought the small, black-muzzled gun from his pocket and pointed it at almost point blank range into the face of the professor. They stood staring into each other's eyes. Perspiration beaded on the face of the older man as he stoically stood his ground and looked into the fanatical eyes of his executioner.

"No," was the quiet reply.

They stood amongst the rain and the thunder. Two, dark figures against a purple and green-tinged sky.

Finally the gun was lowered and thrust back into a pocket.

"So I will find it myself." The man turned and walked away. The discarded implements caught the silver light of a lightning flash and shone briefly.

Professor Bergman waited until he was out of sight and then fell to the ground and vomited into the earth.

***

"What I want to know is this, did he succeed'?" Bob asked, as the four of them sat around a polished table, pints of the dark local brew in front of them. Mannanan, who sat in the corner away from the light and warmth of a bright mullioned window, frowned.

"No."

"Why do I get this distinct impression that he nearly did?" Tavistock asked, taking a sip of lukewarm beer.

"All right, he nearly did," Mannanan agreed, edging further into the shadows.

"But?" Bob asked, looking up and catching Greg's eye.

"You'll have to speak to Sir Arthur, I can't help you any more," Mannanan muttered.

Tavistock and Bob exchanged a look of total exasperation

and when they looked back Mannanan had gone. Greg, sensing his departure, looked from Bob to Tavistock with an air of total incomprehension.

"I don't suppose anyone would care to fill me in? That is if it doesn't come under some sort of local Official Secrets Act?" he asked sarcastically.

"Tavistock, you can do the honours," Bob advised, settling back into his chair, arms folded across his chest.

"As far as I can find out, our absent friend killed, executed or murdered whichever way you look at it, a killer who stalked the Island over a thousand years ago."

"How did he do that?" Greg asked, intrigued.

"He sealed the killer in a cave within a local system of vertical rifts in the cliffs between Port St Mary and Port Erin, known locally as the Chasms. He also sealed in a religious artefact known as the Holy Grail."

"Where the hell did he get that from?" Greg spluttered, convinced that he was now part of some elaborate joke.

"St Patrick," Bob stated flatly, taking a sip of beer.

"Oh." Greg, slowly realising that they were actually being serious, stopped grinning and picked up his pint.

"Apparently St Patrick came to the Island on a visit so secret that it is still cloaked in controversy to this very day. My belief is that he came here with the express desire to hide the Grail, he teemed up with Mannanan and offered him the protection of the holy cup if Mannanan would voluntarily leave the Island or convert to Christianity," Tavistock patiently explained.

"So what did Mannanan do?"

"I think he committed suicide and his spirit was allowed to stay on as a kind of guardian," she added thoughtfully.

"And now when we really need his help he buggers off – bloody typical!"

"Bob!"

"Well. Let's face it, he's not been much good, has he?"

Bob took another swig of beer and wiped the creamy white foam from his upper lip with the back of his hand.

"Well, no," Tavistock agreed, staring down at the table.

"Sent me on a wild goose chase with that bloody awful writer," Bob muttered resentfully.

"I thought you said he'd done it?" Greg argued.

"That was yesterday. Today I find we have a witness who is prepared to go into court and say that our murderer did look like Mr Samuel Lawrence but that he was much younger, slimmer and had distinctive sunken features. Her words by the way, not mine."

"Ah!" Greg and Tavistock declared in unison.

"And that's not all," Bob morosely continued. "According to Brian, our murderer is also an albino as per his message to Tavistock here, received by her a couple of minutes before we arrived at the first dig."

"The DNA test showed certain abnormalities," Tavistock sighed.

"Abnormalities?" Greg asked.

"An extra gene, one which would guarantee that the holder was an albino." Tavistock replied, flicking a beer mat with her fingers.

"White hair, pale skin, reddish eyes, the full works and none of these characteristics are present in Mr Lawrence." Bob grimaced and took another sip of beer. "So we had to let him go. Funny thing is you'd think the guy would have been pleased, but no, he sat in his cell refusing to go."

"Perhaps he liked the food?" Greg chuckled and then suddenly remembering, started guiltily. "Speaking of which, Moira has promised us an abundance of roasted fatted calf if we return before seven."

"Why the hell didn't you say so?" Bob grunted, pushing his beer aside.

"Albino?" Tavistock repeated, a frown of concentration

on her face.

"Yep," Bob said, rising.

"Hang on Bob. I think this may be really important." Tavistock leant forwards in her chair and Bob, exchanging a puzzled look with Greg, sat back down.

"The Glashton."

"Who?" Greg asked.

"The monster, the one incarcerated with the Grail was, according to a parchment found by Professor Bergman, an albino fond of human flesh."

"Argh."

"He apparently ate his victims after raping them."

"What!" Bob, clearly startled, sat rigidly upright as if he'd just been hit by a thunderbolt.

"The Glashton was a cannibal," Tavistock said in the tones of a teacher with a particularly thick pupil.

"I know what a cannibal is, thank you," Bob retorted stung. "What you didn't know was that Chelsea had bite marks on her neck and breasts – quite large ones, inflicted, the pathologist believes, just before she was thrown into the water."

"Good God!" Greg breathed, his eyes widening in disbelief.

"Perhaps this is another copycat crime and some mad bugger reckons he's the Glashton incarnate," Bob muttered. "But who?"

"And why?" Greg muttered, stroking his chin thoughtfully.

"Mannanan reckons someone has found the cave where he imprisoned the monster and that for some reason the Glashton is now stronger in spirit and is just waiting to get out again," Tavistock said.

"Sounds like some daft horror film script," Greg moaned.

"Aye it does, which makes me still feel that we may

be on the right track with our film writer," Bob muttered thoughtfully.

"But where does Ian Felton-Cholmondley come in?" Tavistock asked. "And why has our elderly friend been so keen to muddy the waters? Besides I felt something when I was on the beach with Gloria, something truly evil and definitely not human."

They sat in silence for a few minutes, each with their own thoughts.

"First thing tomorrow we go and see Sir Arthur and tell him everything. I have a horrible feeling what we have now is a repeat of something which happened over fifty years ago and that for whatever reason Sir Arthur knows more than he's telling," Bob reasoned, coming to a decision.

"You know something else, I reckon he made some sort of bargain with our mutual friend for the good of the Island. Mannanan was far too keen to not let me find a receipt for a boat trip Professor Bergman made when he first arrived here," Tavistock added.

"And he's been very reticent about the whole Glashton thing. Totally different to last year," Bob said, thought processes spinning wildly as he considered various anomalies, which had at the time made no sense whatsoever.

They sat again in silence. The mobile in Tavistock's bag buzzed in bad temper. Answering it, Tavistock looked across at Bob and mouthed 'Moira'. She listened, a grin growing with every second that passed. Finally she said. "Yes, I'll certainly tell him". And then switched the mobile phone off.

"That was Moira. She says if you don't come home in half an hour, your dinner will be in the dog."

"We don't have a dog," Bob said, a puzzled frown on his features.

"I gather she's thinking of trading you in," Tavistock

replied. "And before you ask, yes, I'll be at Sir Arthur's tomorrow morning at ten o'clock to listen to more memoirs."

"Right, see you there then. Come on Greg, we'd better be off. I'm in the doghouse already without having to build it too. Although knowing Moira I'm sure that by now she's already ordered the wood."

They all laughed and collecting their things, left the smoke-filled confines of the pub for the bright golden sunshine of the outside world.

***

Samuel Lawrence stood in front of his bedroom mirror and stared hard at his reflection. From across the room the shrill voice of madness started its soft whining again.

"I got you out didn't I?"

"Leave me alone."

"You made me a promise. A promise I intend you to keep," the voice spat into his ear.

"I can't – not any more. I gave you the boy and then the girl. I can't do any more. I don't want to do any more!" A tear trickled down his face, haggard and grey.

"I need your help one last time, and then it will all be over. You get what you want and I get what I want," the voice whispered persuasively.

"I can't, I won't!" Samuel Lawrence tried to turn away but found himself almost pinned to the glass.

"You can and you will."

Eyes, red-rimmed and glinting, stared back at him. Finally he backed down and fell to the floor.

"All right, all right, I'll do it – just leave me alone. Leave me alone!" he sobbed, and clawed at the carpet. "Leave me alone, just leave me alone." Sobs wracked his body until finally, exhausted, he fell into an unquiet sleep.

***

Caroline and Brian sat on either side of their dining table and glared at the large sheet of paper in front of them.

"Well, that's the top table sorted. You, me, Bob, Moira and two bridesmaids," Caroline yawned, sitting back and rubbing her eyes.

"Perhaps we could put your mother with mine and stick them on the end next to Moira?" Brian asked, writing their names down on the rectangle of paper in front of him.

"Then we could put your father and Edna on the other end next to Bob." Caroline remarked. "That way your mother doesn't have to talk to either and my mother has a captive audience for her anti-male comments. Just a minute, how many does that make?"

Brian carefully counted the names on his list and exhaled miserably. "Ten."

"Ten? Are you sure?"

"Yes."

"Oh God, that means two will have to go."

"Couldn't we sit on another table?" Brian asked hopefully.

"No, but what about if we have a finger buffet? Then we let people sit where they want!" Caroline looked across at him with a wicked glint in her eye.

"And we would then have one of the shortest receptions in history, as they would actually be within thumping distance of each other." He looked despondently down on the list. "Why don't we just rearrange the tables and have one very long top table with say twenty on it and lots of little ones, underneath?"

"Brilliant – now all we have to do is chose ten people who get on with either my mother or your father."

"How about sticking my sister Isabelle next to your mother and Moira? We can say it's so she can keep an eye on her daughter Poppy, bridesmaid number two."

"What about Andy?"

"What about him?" Brian asked with a puzzled frown.

"He can't stand your mother; if he sits anywhere near her, after one glass of wine it will be pistols at dawn."

"Really?"

"Brian, the last time we went round there he said she was a vitriolic, evil-minded old bat!"

"Ah, perhaps we could put him down the other end."

"He also said that the only intelligent thing she'd ever done was to leave your father!"

"Right. Do you think he'd mind sitting on his own?" Brian asked. Caroline gave him the sort of look his mother usually reserved for congenital idiots and crossed his sister's name off the list.

"I have a better idea, why don't we just run away to Jamaica and send everyone a boxed set of wedding photographs?" Caroline muttered, running tired fingers through her hair.

"Bob!" Brian succinctly uttered.

"Ah!" Caroline looked down at the long list of names they were planning to invite and felt like crying. Why oh why did families have to have so many silly feuds, and why were they all coming to her wedding? Suddenly she looked up and fixing Brian with a mutinous look, said, "Right, well if good old Uncle Bob wants us to get married here then he can sort out the seating plan, I'm going to bed!"

Chapter 11

Mona Erskine pressed the intercom button and wrapped herself more tightly in her fine Egyptian cotton bathtowel.

"Who is it?" she barked into the metal mouthpiece.

"Only me," came the succinct reply.

"What do you want?" Mona asked, suddenly suspicious.

"Just a friendly chat, that's all," came the reply.

"Why?"

"Why not. Oh, come, on, Sisi, open up. I need a gin and tonic."

"Ice and a slice," Mona laughed and pressed the button to open the gate.

She could see him walking up the drive, head bent, gravel crunching and spurting from the heavy black boots he habitually wore. Sally ran towards him and then five yards from his striding figure she sat abruptly and sniffed the air. The growl that emanated from her small furry throat caused even the hairs on Mona's neck to stand upright. Sally, yellow teeth bared in a snarl, suddenly attacked as the man reached the door and Mona, furious with the dog, threw the heavy oak door open to shout at the animal now clinging grimly to one boot.

"Get off him, you stupid mutt," she said, trying to hold

onto her bathrobe and prise open the animal's jaws at the same time.

"Just kick her," she added, standing up and pulling the towelling cloth back up over large sagging breasts. The skin wrinkled like crepe bandages still wet and studded with soap-suds.

"Be glad to," the man muttered, kicking out at the dog still clinging to the hem of his trousers. Sally fell back onto the brick surface of the front steps, blood spurting from a deep cut on her soft black upper lip.

Mona looked at the man, his face half hidden by a velvet-edged hat brim and wrinkled her forehead in distaste.

"Why on earth do you still insist on wearing that ridiculous thing?" she asked, standing to one side as he sidled past her.

The man looked around the house and chuckled. Mona, in the act of shutting the door, frowned.

"Are you all right? You sound odd."

"I'm all right." The man removed the hat and stared down at her and Mona screamed.

"Where's Sam?" she shouted, now thoroughly frightened. "What have you done with him?"

"Nothing. I've done nothing with him. I just need to know where something is."

"What?" Mona asked, desperately looking around her for a way out.

"The letter." The man suddenly grabbed her around the throat and thrust her up against the hall wall. Mona, feeling his weight against her, and something hardening between her large thighs, began to sob hysterically.

"I don't know what you mean."

"Oh yes you do. The letter your father left you in his will. The old illuminated manuscript. The book of runes."

"Oh that."

"Yes that." He looked down on her and smiled slyly.

"I sold it."

"What?" he exploded, abruptly letting her go.

"You stupid, stupid little man, where did you think the money for all this came from?" Mona, breathing hard, spat at him, mean triumph showing for a second deep within her eyes. Spotting the look, the man hit her in the face.

Later, when he'd finished, he pulled the borrowed clothes back on and sat back thoughtfully on a green wicker recliner.

There was only one way out now and for that he would need a certain amount of help from someone who was in even more desperate need than he was himself.

Quietly he let himself out of the house and walked slowly down the drive to the gate at the end. Hiding his face with the wide brim of the hat, he waved to Harold. Harold, returning from the local shop, slowed the Mercedes to let the man past and frowned. He hadn't been aware that Mona was expecting a visitor. Carefully he parked in the drive and opened the door. It was then that he heard the soft plaintive whimpering.

"Sally? Sally?" he called, earnestly searching for his pet.

Sally stumbled from the clump of Sweet Williams where she had managed to drag herself to after the attack and crawled towards him. Her muzzle was covered in blood, a tooth embedded through the soft velvet underlip sticking out at a grotesque angle. Harold ran to her and gently picked her up. The dog screamed in pain and Harold lowered her gently back down onto the soft grass.

Anger washing over him he hurled himself at the car and after a few fumbling seconds found his mobile phone. He dialled 999 and waited.

The police found him minutes later huddled up outside his own front door cradling the unconscious animal in his hands.

Bob and Brian arrived fifteen minutes after that, their faces set in lines etched with worry. It was Harold who let the young police constable inside and Harold who had discovered his wife's bloody remains floating face down in their blue-tiled swimming pool.

Bob sat on the other side of Harold's shrunken figure and searched for the right words. Brian silently handed Harold a large mug of hot sweet tea and sat beside him.

"Do you have any idea who the man was?" Bob gently asked.

"No, not really. I think he came round before a few weeks ago."

"The vet just rang," Brian informed him gently. "He says that Sally will be fine. She needs rest and a lot of TLC but in a few weeks she'll be back to digging up the garden and chasing cats."

Harold gave a small shattered smile and then shuddered.

"How, how did she die?" he asked.

"We don't know as yet," Bob replied, his features set. Brian knew that look only too well; it was one Bob reserved for the relatives of a violent death.

"Sir." A young police constable handed Bob a sheaf of recently developed photographs. Bob, startled, looked at the top one and swore softly.

"Was this the man?" he asked, handing the photograph to Harold. Harold peered at it and nodded, tears running down his face.

Bob stood up and walked rapidly from the room, issuing a series of instructions as he went.

"Brian, get hold of whichever idiot is currently not tailing Mr Lawrence and have him thrown off the nearest cliff. Duncan, you and Peter there can arrest Mr Lawrence as of now. Juan, get hold of Mr Erskine's GP and stay with him until his friend turns up."

Bob Callow was still talking to Seth Riley when Duncan called from Samuel Lawrence's house. Bob listened carefully, his face darkening as Duncan described in graphic detail exactly what he had found. Brian stood and watched him, waiting for the explosion.

"That was young Duncan, he's just found young Constable Collister unconscious behind a wheely bin at the back of Mr Lawrence's holiday flat. He's phoned for an ambulance but as one side of the face of our young Sherlock Homes has been smashed in he doesn't hold out much hope of any intelligent information from that particular source for some considerable time. Mr Lawrence, as you might expect, is nowhere to be seen and while he was waiting for the ambulance, Anne Swales called round. And this is the really juicy bit – the real icing on the cake. A small amount of explosive together with a set of fuses and some sort of timing mechanism has gone missing from their special effects department. Which one of you would like to make an educated guess as to whom was caught on camera taking them? Our friend Mr Samuel Lawrence! Can this day get any worse?"

Brian shuffled from one foot to the other and cleared his throat nervously.

"Well, out with it!" Bob growled at him.

"We've just had a call from the Met. Ian Felton-Cholmondley has vanished and they think he may be on his way here."

"And just exactly why do they think that?"

"Because the last call he made from his personal mobile was to a Mr Samuel Lawrence. The call lasted thirteen and a half minutes. He took a taxi to a small private airport just outside London. The pilot he had hired dropped him off at Caernarfon and from there he appears to have hired another taxi and then a boat from Bangor. That was the last anyone has actually seen of him."

"This boat, big enough to get here?"

"Oh yes. According to the local police it has enough fuel to get to Ireland which is where they thought at first he was heading."

"Great, just great. We have one nutter running around with what amounts to a do-it-yourself bomb kit and a missing politician who may or may not be involved in a spate of blackmail, rape and murder. My cup, young Brian, fairly runneth over."

"So what do we do now?"

"Do? I tell you what we are going to do. We are going to get a set of very nasty high voltage electrodes out of mothballs. After which we will find Sir Arthur bleeding Felton and apply said electrodes to certain key areas of elderly flesh until he starts telling us the truth, the whole truth and nothing but the truth or I shall drag him back to Headquarters and throw away the sodding key!"

***

Bob marched up the drive of the Felton residence and hammered on the door. Sir Arthur, taking one look at his thunderous visage, let him in and followed both Bob Callow and Brian Clague into his study, where Tavistock calmly sat flicking through numerous leather-bound albums.

"And what can I do for you, Detective Inspector?" he politely asked.

"Do? Do?" Bob thundered. "You could start by telling me the truth and you can end by letting me in on whatever it is that you and an elderly relative of mine have been hiding for the past fifty-odd years!"

"I'm sure ..." Sir Arthur's voice tailed off at the bemused expression on Brian's face.

"Don't worry about him, he already thinks I'm one

sandwich short of a picnic anyway."

Brian looked from one to the other and then at Tavistock who shrugged wearily and closed the photograph album.

"I did make a promise once but …"

"I'm well aware of that, I just need to know what it was."

"I'm not sure if …"

"Look, I now have three bodies in the lab, possibly four so I really don't give a damn about some schoolboy sense of decency," Bob declared forcefully.

"I see."

"Four bodies?" Tavistock repeated, visibly shaken.

"The body of Mona Erskine was found an hour ago floating face down in her own swimming pool. She had been savagely sexually assaulted, drowned and then had had large amounts of flesh removed from her upper body. I have every reason to believe that, bizarre as it sounds, someone had tried to eat her. The only plus point was that according to the police surgeon she was already dead and the majority of the attack took place while she was unconscious."

"Good God!" Tavistock and Sir Arthur said in unison.

"So are you going to tell me what exactly happened to the Tidemaster or not?"

"I suppose so, although how it can possibly help you …"

"You tell me what I want to know and I'll judge whether or not it's relevant to my current enquiry," Bob snapped, trying hard to keep his temper under control before sitting down in one of the wing chairs.

"Very well. During the war I was sent here to track down a fascist agent whom we had nicknamed the Tidemaster. I contacted my friend Professor Bergman and he agreed to help me. The professor was at that time working on the remains of a Viking longboat. Within those remains he found references to a book, written just after the supposed visit of St Patrick to this island. The book turned out to be an illuminated manuscript, which set out the legend of the Glashton, a cannibal thrown off the shores of Ireland by the local early monks. It referred to the ancient God Mannanan Mac Lir and to a pact that he made with St Patrick and to ancient runes or chants, which were used to incarcerate the Glashton in an underground chamber. The professor's main interest was that the Holy Grail had been left within the cave to both protect the Island and itself from being used by less scrupulous men. Professor Bergman found the cave but didn't feel able to enter."

"Why not?" Bob asked, somewhat more calmly as his blood pressure slowly approached its usual level.

"He said he had such a sense of evil that he couldn't breathe."

"Ah." Bob and Tavistock exchanged identical glances of understanding.

"What happened to the manuscript?" Tavistock asked.

"As far as I know it was stolen. At the time I thought that the Tidemaster had it. The riot in the barracks at Douglas Promenade happened a day after the book went missing. I remember looking at the flames and knowing that my man was involved with causing it."

"So what did you do?"

"I made a bargain with the God Mannanan."

"What sort of bargain?" Bob asked uneasily.

"I would hide or destroy any evidence that suggested that the Grail or the Glashton existed if he would ensure that the Tidemaster never met up with his masters."

"And why did you want to do that?"

"There were things happening to young girls in the south of the Island."

"Such as?" Bob asked, even though he had a fair idea now as to what it might have been.

"Three girls disappeared, they all knew the man I thought

of as the Tidemaster. Each disappearance coincided with a low tide and there were witnesses that swore each time that my suspect had been with them. He of course denied it and his alibi was always the same. Basically that he was an internee and not able to have been anywhere with the girls in question. The bodies were never found, although we did find what we believed was an arm of one of the unfortunate young women. It was found on rocks down by the Chasms by a local fisherman and – strange as it seemed at the time – looked as though it had been gnawed away from the rest of the body. To be honest I still have nightmares to this day over what happened to those poor creatures. One evening I took a boat and approached the cliffs near where the limb had been found and I discovered the cave entrance. I have never felt such malignancy, such hatred, emanating from the very rocks themselves." Sir Arthur paused, his face white and drawn. Shakily, he crossed himself. Brian shivered and wondered if it was his imagination that was making him feel suddenly so cold.

"I actually wondered if somehow the spirit or soul of the monster was somehow still alive."

"Or maybe someone had let the Glashton out?"

"That or they were acting as the Glashton would have if he'd still been alive."

"So what did you do?" Brian asked.

"I took some sticks of dynamite from stores and blew the entrance of the cave system up. I thought I had sealed it for all eternity. The day afterwards the riot started and then we found the remains of our agent, burned alive."

"Only you didn't believe it was him?"

"No, no I didn't."

"Why?"

"I really have no idea, call it intuition or a hunch – whatever, I had this feeling that he was still out there waiting. That was when I made my bargain with Mannanan. I sat hunched up above what I believed was the Glashton's lair and I waited. It was late evening when he came scurrying across the rocks, on all fours like some sort of hideous parody of a spider or a crab. I remember he reached the place where I'd set the charges and he screamed. I could see him tearing at the entrance and then I approached him. He looked up at me and our eyes met. I shall never forget those eyes. They were red, Inspector, and lurking within their depths I caught a glimpse of the man who I had once called my enemy, 'The Tidemaster'."

"What did you do?"

"I shot him at point blank range."

"And?" Bob urged him on.

"I held him in my arms as he died. I shall never forget his last words to me, they will haunt me for the rest of my life." Sir Arthur paused for breath, his hands shaking as he clutched at the sides of his chair.

"He said, 'Thank you,' and then he died. The tide took him afterwards. They never found the body and to this day I've never told a single soul."

"And the murders of the young girls?" Brian asked.

"They stopped as suddenly as they had started, the enquiry was dropped and all those connected with it either died or gradually forgot."

"And now it's all started again," Bob said, standing up and moving to the window.

"Do you believe in possession, Inspector?" Sir Arthur asked. Bob turned to face him and their eyes met and held.

"I didn't, no," Bob replied.

"Neither did I up until that point. I asked a priest afterwards what he thought."

"And what did he say?" Bob stared at him, an oddly reflective look on his face.

"He said that in certain circumstances he could believe

that someone could become so obsessed with a particular being that he could become that person, even down to the point of looking like him."

"Nonsense," Brian muttered.

"You think so?" Sir Arthur paused thoughtfully before continuing almost as if he were weighing him up. "Have you ever noticed how people who have been together for a very long time and know each other so well actually end up looking like each other?"

There was a brief, thought-filled silence.

"Moira, that's the wife, is heavily into the old amateur dramatics and she says that when you live with a character for any length of time, to really give a good performance you end up becoming it. She reckons that that is a kind of possession." Bob mused aloud.

"But that's just acting!" Brian exclaimed.

"Is it?" Tavistock asked. "Writers do it too sometimes, they can become so obsessed with a character that they can actually change their own personalities. Perhaps if someone were researching the part of the Glashton, they could actually believe that they were ..."

"What?" Bob exclaimed, a startled look of understanding settling on his features. "Brian, do you remember in Samuel Lawrence's apartment he had all those books about legends and ..."

"There were masses of them, some looked to me like they ought to belong in a museum." Brian sat up. "But you don't seriously think that ..." he added, looking from one to the other.

"Come on, we have to get back there and find out where he is in his research. No hang on – you go dig around and ring me if you find anything, Sir Arthur, I've a map in the car – show me exactly where this cave is."

"Certainly, if you think it will help."

"I'm willing to bet Samuel Lawrence has found it

already."

"You think he could be hiding out there?" Tavistock asked.

"At the moment I'd put money on it," Bob snapped grimly.

"Tavistock you can drive me in your car, I'll ring the coastguard and order a boat. Brian, ring me as soon as you find anything at all, however daft it might seem – anything, you understand?"

"Yes Boss."

Sir Arthur, after pointing out the position of the Glashton's lair, stood in the rays of a hot summer sun and for the first time in over fifty years prayed that this time it would really be all over.

Chapter 12

Brian hastily poured hot water into the thermos flask in front of him and screwed on the cap. It could, he thought, be a long night. He was just extracting the last packet of chocolate biscuits from the cupboard above his head when the door to their flat opened and Caroline walked in.

"What are you doing?" she asked, her face growing pale as she half guessed the correct answer.

"We think we know who the murderer is and we have a good idea where he is currently holed up," Brian told her, pushing the flask and the biscuits into a small canvas bag.

"Holed up as in cornered, as in cornered rat?" Caroline enquired nervously.

"Something like that," Brian muttered, grabbing the bag and making for the door.

"Are we talking dangerous and cornered here?" Caroline asked, blocking the doorway with her body.

"Maybe," Brian agreed, and then added on seeing the suddenly haunted look in her eyes, "but Bob will be with me and he's called in the marksmen so …"

"Guns!" Caroline exploded. "Marksmen! And that's supposed to make me feel better!"

"Caroline love …"

"Don't you love me? Just go, go." She moved aside then, tears brightly glinting in her eyes.

Brian suddenly distressed by her obvious terror, took

her in his arms and kissed her, feeling her cling to him at first and then, as she became calmer push him away.

"Go, and don't do anything daft."

"No, Mum," he replied, his mood suddenly lightening.

"Mum!" she muttered angrily after he'd gone and she began to prepare her own solitary meal. "Mum!"

***

Bob sat in the bottom of the boat and peered over the side at the approaching cliffs. Slate, shale and white-streaked granite hung suspended above his head. He felt as though he was being pressed down, a tiny piece of unimportant flotsam, to be played with by the tide and wind.

"How the bloody hell do people make a living out here?" he muttered to Brian crouched in the stern. Brian, going quietly green around the gills, refused to answer.

"Could be blowing up for a bit of a storm," the helmsman told them as he stared out at the approaching black and purple clouds hugging the horizon in a thick ominous band.

"Great!" Bob exclaimed. "Even the bloody weather's against me!"

"Not necessarily." Cora, who was pinpointing their current position on a well-thumbed chart, observed. "It will just mean that if anyone is in this cave they won't be able to get out."

"Oh." Bob smiled, suddenly much happier than he had been for the past hour.

Brian groaned again and retched drily into the water that was frothing and foaming around the small but very fast craft.

Bob ignored him and concentrated on the cliffs above them; he could see a creeping movement as men on ropes swung perilously as they tried to get a better grip. Police marksmen were positioning themselves at strategic points, their lines of sight taking in the entrance of the cave and its paths to and from the sea.

Finally they spotted it, a dark gap in the cold grey slabs and ripples of rock. Water boiled and bubbled from underneath and Brian stared at Bob with a look of absolute terror.

"You never said anything about an underground entrance!"

"Didn't I?" Bob asked innocently.

"No you bloody well didn't!"

"Now, now, language."

"You know I get claustrophobic," Brian muttered.

"What, a big bloke like you?" Bob replied, a grin settling around his lips.

Brian continued muttering until Bob, feeling that the joke had gone far enough, pointed to a spot just to the left of the entrance. A black glossy head bobbed up from the water and started to move towards them. After a few minutes black-gloved hands grasped the side of the boat and the rubber-suited frogman was hauled inside.

"Well, Jim?" Bob asked.

"Nobody there at the moment but someone's been in recently. There was a flask in one corner and some kind of wicker box; I presumed it was a picnic basket of some sort. There were a few items of clothing and a sleeping bag wrapped up in a plastic binliner. And something you might not like, considering why we are here, but there was an assortment of bones in one corner."

"Bones?"

"Aye, and I wouldn't want to put any money on some of them not being human."

"Ah." Bob sighed.

"So what do you want us to do?" Cora asked.

"We find some sort of vantage point where we can hide

without being easily seen and we wait," Bob said. "Cora, can you get on the radio and let everyone know that this could be a very long night?"

Up above on the clifftop amongst the rough grass and thorny miniature roses that clung to the windswept edges, Tavistock and Mannanan stood anxiously side by side and waited.

"Can't you do anything?" Tavistock whispered.

"Maybe," Mannanan whispered.

"Well, go on then"

"If I get caught for interfering ..." Mannanan let the words hang in the air between them. Tavistock, suddenly furious, rounded on him.

"Interfering? What the hell do you call what you did last year then?"

"I didn't do anything?"

"No, you just left your lady friend to sort it out."

"She's no friend of mine," Mannanan hissed back.

"No?"

"No!"

Tavistock gave a snort of derision and turned her back on him.

"No wonder women have an affinity for cats, they are just like them!" Mannanan observed angrily.

"We can't just stand here and do nothing, someone might get hurt," Tavistock uttered despairingly.

"Good." Mannanan retorted, thinking about how much he'd like to see his old enemy laid out on a grey slab with a modern bullet between the eyes.

"I meant either Bob or Brian," Tavistock retorted.

"Ah."

"Bob says Samuel has a fair amount of explosive on him and they think Ian Felton has a firearm of some sort."

"Oh?" Mannanan watched her, his eyes showing the uneasiness he was beginning to feel.

"His grandfather rang to say that the gun cabinet had been forced open but someone had reset the burglar alarm afterwards. Ian apparently had the code numbers."

"Ah." Mannanan looked thoughtfully at her and then shuffled uneasily.

"I suppose if you came with me it wouldn't then be me doing the interfering," he added.

"What?" Tavistock turned, fear and shock vying for supremacy.

"All you have to do is hold my hand, close your eyes and repeat what I say."

"Repeat what you say?"

"Exactly. Here we go then."

Tavistock felt her hand gripped and quickly closed her eyes, repeating the old and ancient words almost in a trance.

***

Duncan, wandering across the turf from the car park, now taped off and full of empty vehicles, stopped and looked around. Carefully and more than slightly puzzled he spoke quietly into his radio.

"It's me Duncan, Tavistock Allan has gone sir ... I don't know where although I could have sworn she was standing here only minutes ago ... Yes if I see her I'll tell her." Duncan sank down onto the grass to wait and huddled further into his dark thick anorak; the air was dropping in temperature as the cloud mass of heavy rain approached. Flashes of lightning briefly flared across the sea as the ominous growl of thunder rolled along the surface of the waves, growing nearer with each minute that ticked by.

Tavistock opened her eyes and shuddered. The cave stretched around her, a faint glow emanating from slivers of wood piled on top of a low ledge carved naturally into the rock wall.

Around them they could feel a chilling, dank atmosphere of salt-laden air and something oppressively wrong. It was the feeling of wrongness that caused Tavistock to look around nervously until finally she spotted it crouched in the corner, hugging the weed-laden sides.

Finally after what seemed like hours, there was a sound of water splashing against rock and a figure emerged cautiously from the pool of dark ripples guarding the underground entrance.

A few minutes later another clambered up from the depths and stood shivering in the gloom until one of the figures lit a small hurricane lamp. The harsh white light split the gloom with such suddenness that Tavistock was almost blinded.

"Where is it then?" Ian Felton-Cholmondley asked.

"Up there, on the shelf," his companion replied.

"What, this heap of sawdust?" Ian spat.

"That's all that's left. What did you expect, some sort of glowing golden chalice worked with rubies and other precious stones?" Samuel openly sneered.

"Then if that's all that's left why bring me here?"

"Why indeed?" Samuel muttered. Tavistock and Ian both stared at him, puzzled. The voice sounded odd, almost as if it belonged to someone else. Tavistock, still clutching Mannanan's hand, looked to him for reassurance. Mannanan silently shook his head and laid a cold bony finger on her lips.

"What do you mean?"

"Mean – what could I possibly mean?"

"You, you sound different." Ian, now beginning to experience the sort of fear he normally caused in others, began to back slowly towards the gently lapping water. Outside the storm strengthened, sending sheets of wind scurrying across the surface of the sea.

"Oh I wouldn't do that if I were you. You see this?" Samuel, bending down, picked up a small black box from the floor of the cave and straightening up again, walked towards the now thoroughly frightened politician.

"Yes. What ... what is it?" Ian nervously licked his lips, a combination of perspiration and saltwater slowly beading on his skin.

"This is a switch. Quite a simple thing really. You just turn this little knob here and boom!"

"Boom?"

"Boom. We are sealed in forever."

"Sealed?" Ian shuddered and took a step back, cold water licked at his feet, darting sharp icy serpent tongues at his toes.

"Yes, sealed." The voice now clearly triumphant continued. "I've planted explosives at the entrance in strategic places. When it goes the whole of this cave system will collapse and we will be locked in here for all eternity. Or at least our poor lost souls will be."

"Who are you?"

"Samuel Lawrence, man of letters but I'm afraid to say not much else."

"No I mean – who are you really?"

"And I thought you'd never ask." Slowly the face of Samuel Lawrence changed, features blurred as the sharp bone structure of the Glashton poked through the tightening, greying skin. Eyes red-rimmed and glinting watched from a face transformed.

"What are you?" Ian whispered, his lips trembling with fear and his whole body seized in a vice-like grip of pure terror.

"I am the Glashton, the protector of the thing you and your father before you have wanted so very badly."

"Why me?" Ian asked, his voice a terrified whisper.

"Revenge!"

"Revenge? What have I ever done to you?" Ian exclaimed.

"Nothing," the Glashton snapped, moving back towards the wall and squatting on an upturned wooden pallet.

"Then?"

"Your grandfather killed me. No, let me finish. Or rather, he killed my way out of here."

"I don't understand, how?"

"You really aren't all that bright, are you?" the Glashton sneered, showing his teeth in a wicked parody of a smile. "It really is quite simple really, I am dead. You are alive. I take over your body, your youth and I live. That heap of wood was the Grail. In a few more years even the dust will have blown away and I will be of no further use. If I don't get out of here soon, I will simply cease to be. I have guarded it faithfully; no one has removed or even touched it. And do you know how they thank me, do you?" He moved closer to the man he was to possess and breathed the stench of death into his face. Ian gagged and fell to the ground, dislodging stones and bones in a clatter of sound. "They will send me to oblivion. That oh-so-holy man and his sycophant."

"What can I do?"

"You can repair the wrong your grandfather did me and become my vessel. I will live in you and you in me."

"And Samuel?"

"Samuel will stay here and when we have gone he will press the button and boom!"

"But the police ..."

"Saw you enter with Mr Lawrence. There will be a fight over the cup, over money. He will attack you, you will fight back and escape and he, while insane, will kill himself. All you have to do is play your part."

"I won't, I can't." Ian stared madness in the face and then did the bravest thing he had ever done; he tried to wrest the black box from the calloused hands of Samuel Lawrence. Something flickered in the depths of Samuel's eyes as he tried desperately to help.

Mannanan watched and then moved towards the struggling men. Tavistock, released from her lethargy, stumbled forwards. She made a grab at Ian and then half pulled, half pushed him into the water. "Go!" she hissed. Ian, shocked at suddenly seeing her, nevertheless nodded briefly and then dived into the gloomy depths.

Mannanan struggled with the man they had once known as Samuel Lawrence and finally flung the box to the ground. Tavistock bent and retrieved it. The Glashton, trembling, ran a bony hand across his face and screamed in frustration.

"You!"

"Yes, I."

"I want to leave, that's all. Haven't I been punished enough? I want to taste the sky and feel the sun on my own skin!"

"I know," Mannanan suddenly looking like the old man he truly was, reached out a hand in something akin to pity. Slowly releasing his grasp on the frail body of Samuel Lawrence, the Glashton shimmered towards him.

"Go, take the old fool with you, hurry," a voice inside Tavistock's head urged.

Turning swiftly, she grabbed the writer and tugged him away from the wall, forcing him into the ice-cold sea.

Grabbing a lungful of air she followed; seconds later she emerged and strong hands lifted her up and onto the slabs of rock at the base of the cliffs.

"Have to get everyone away – explosives!" she tried to shout, her voice hoarse and breathy.

***

Huddled next to Bob and wrapped in a silver foil-lined blanket, she watched, spellbound as the night air was split apart by a bright flash of orange and white. Rock groaned and screamed as it released its grip and billowed and scuttled into the sea. White foam spat and hissed as it received the lumps and boulders of slate and stone. Until finally all was swallowed up. The outline of the towering cliffs changed forever in just a few brief moments.

Samuel Lawrence shuffled between his guard of two grim-faced policemen and hummed. His eyes finally dulled by madness stared unseeing as they drove him off.

He would, Bob thought, without much joy, spend the remainder of his years in some bright hospital ward, drugged to the eyeballs and dead to the world around him.

Tavistock watched him go as she stood side by side with Ian Felton-Cholmondley, who had at the last been prepared to give his life for the sake of the Island, as had his grandfather before him. Part of her hoped that there might now be a small slim chance of reconciliation between the two men if only for the sake of the woman they both loved in their own very different ways, her old friend Constance.

She sighed. Maybe something good would come of it all, eventually. She closed her eyes and again saw that brief image of Mannanan holding a slim frightened youth in his arms.

"So what happens now?" she asked Bob as they made their weary way along the breakwater.

"We book Samuel Lawrence for the murders of Barney Goldsmith, Chelsea Thomas and Mona Erskine. Mind you, I doubt that he'll go to prison. They'll say he was obsessed with an old legend and killed while the balance of his mind etc ... Mind you, it will be the first time I'll actually be pleased to see one of them potty psychologists in court."

"But ..."

"Look, I might believe in the old stories of possession but do you honestly believe the courts will?"

"No."

"Besides in a way he did bring it upon himself."

"And Ian?" Tavistock tentatively asked as he was escorted to a waiting car by yet more grimly unsmiling police officers.

"Will get a slap on the wrist and will lose his job." Bob drily observed. "Or at least with any luck he will," he added.

"Well what do you want me to do?" Brian asked, catching them up.

"Do? You can go in and sort out the paperwork and I'm going back to bed."

"But ..." Brian whined plaintively.

"I'm on holiday lad, remember? Tavistock, have you got your car love? Because I could do with a lift. As Brian will be needing his to get back to Headquarters."

Bob grinned, stuffed his hands in his pockets and ambled off.

***

Brian carefully and very quietly opened the door of his flat and not daring to switch on the light in case he woke Caroline, made his way in the dim half-light of the street lamp outside, towards the kitchen.

A table lamp was switched on, bathing him in a sudden pool of yellow light.

"Well?" Caroline asked from her temporary bed on the sofa. "What happened?"

Brian walked tiredly towards her and sat himself down beside her on the sofa before replying, his voice slow and blurred with cold and lack of sleep.

"We got him. No one was hurt and we even managed to re-design the coastline in the process, which ..." he added with an attempt at humour. "Will probably come out of my wages."

Caroline snuggled up next to him, pressing her warm semi-naked body up against his cold shivering bulk.

"Good, I would hate to have to continuously hold up a picture of Daddy to our firstborn." Brian stared at her in silent horror as she blithely continued.

"Much better to have the real thing wandering in and out, making the odd mess, painting the odd wall ..."

Brian continued to stare, his eyes almost standing out on stalks.

"You mean ... I'm going to be a dad?"

"Yes." Caroline smoothed the curling hair back from behind his ears. "Do you mind?" she asked, suddenly nervous.

"Mind, mind? Of course I don't mind. Whatever made you say that?" he asked, his voice rough with concern.

"Well you've never actually ... I mean we have never really discussed children."

"Because I didn't know whether we could have any, after last year, and I couldn't talk about it. It was enough just to have you," he admitted.

"Oh!" Caroline breathed, suddenly seeing the truth and loving him even more for it.

"I love you," she whispered into his ear. "And ..." she added huskily. "I'd love you even more if you would only come to bed and get a decent night's sleep for once."

Chapter 13

Bob Callow lay on the white, sun-drenched sand and sighed contentedly.

'This is the life eh?' he thought, grinning. 'Sun, sea, sand, palm trees, unlimited buffets of food and absolutely nothing to remind me of home.' He had even managed to get into Moira's good books by booking the holiday himself and leaving her nothing to do but to pack.

It wasn't often you got the chance of a direct flight holiday from the Island especially at such short notice.

He was still basking in his own glory when a small child's voice asked, "Uncle Bob, Uncle Mac says he's too hot to play with me and Mummy's asleep so wouldn't you like to go swimming?"

Bob groaned and screwed his eyes into slits. George Allan stood over him, gently dripping and smiling happily.

"Did you say Uncle Mac?" Bob tentatively asked.

"Yes?" George replied, faintly puzzled.

"I thought," Bob paused, searching for the right words and remembering what Tavistock had told him about the battle in the cave, "that Uncle Mac was dead."

"Oh he is," George agreed, giving him an oddly grown-up look.

"Then why, if he's dead, does he need a holiday?"

"Because even dead people need a rest," George replied with all the wisdom of the average seven-year-old.